"Boss is really on ⟨...⟩
the kidnapper said.

Tess shrugged. The idiot ⟨...⟩
was standing right next to them. "He gets that
way. You know how it is. You don't expect
somebody in his position to be kind, generous,
or go way beyond the call for his people."

All of which Josh Redstone was and did, and if
these clowns had done their homework they'd
have known that. And for just an instant as Josh
himself looked at her, she saw acknowledgment
of the compliment she'd just indirectly paid him.

Not that it wasn't anything she hadn't said to
him directly before; he knew quite well she
thought the world of him.

He just didn't know she was in love with him,
and had been for a very long time.

Become a fan of Silhouette Romantic Suspense
books on Facebook and check us out at
www.eHarlequin.com!

Dear Reader,

REDSTONE, INCORPORATED didn't begin as a series. I'd written the first book, *Just Another Day in Paradise,* without any idea there might be more. But by the time I got to the end, the idea had been born. Still, I had no idea I would be living in the Redstone world for more than nine years. I thought a trilogy, or at most maybe a half dozen books, would do it. But the scope of Redstone grew, and the opportunities for stories I wanted to tell multiplied, until at last we're at an even dozen.

To all the readers who have made this journey with me, I say thank you so very much. Without you, obviously, this world would never have existed and survived for so long.

But it's finally time to leave. And of course the only way to do that is to give the center of that world, the core character who made it all work, his own happy ending. No one deserves it more.

So, Josh my friend—by now my *old* friend—here you are. Enjoy that flight into the sunset. You've earned it.

Justine Davis

JUSTINE DAVIS

Redstone Ever After

ROMANTIC
SUSPENSE

If you purchased this book without a cover you should be aware
that this book is stolen property. It was reported as "unsold and
destroyed" to the publisher, and neither the author nor the
publisher has received any payment for this "stripped book."

SILHOUETTE BOOKS

Recycling programs
for this product may
not exist in your area.

ISBN-13: 978-0-373-27689-9

REDSTONE EVER AFTER

Copyright © 2010 by Janice Davis Smith

All rights reserved. Except for use in any review, the reproduction
or utilization of this work in whole or in part in any form by any
electronic, mechanical or other means, now known or hereafter
invented, including xerography, photocopying and recording, or in
any information storage or retrieval system, is forbidden without
the written permission of the editorial office, Silhouette Books,
233 Broadway, New York, NY 10279 U.S.A.

This is a work of fiction. Names, characters, places and incidents are
either the product of the author's imagination or are used fictitiously, and
any resemblance to actual persons, living or dead, business establishments,
events or locales is entirely coincidental.

This edition published by arrangement with Harlequin Books S.A.

For questions and comments about the quality of this book
please contact us at Customer_eCare@Harlequin.ca.

® and TM are trademarks of Harlequin Books S.A., used under license.
Trademarks indicated with ® are registered in the United States Patent
and Trademark Office, the Canadian Trade Marks Office and in other
countries.

Visit Silhouette Books at www.eHarlequin.com

Printed in U.S.A.

Books by Justine Davis

Silhouette Romantic Suspense

Lover Under Cover #698
Leader of the Pack #728
A Man to Trust #805
Gage Butler's Reckoning #841
Badge of Honor #871
Clay Yeager's Redemption #926
The Return of Luke McGuire #1036
**Just Another Day
  in Paradise #1141
The Prince's Wedding #1190
**One of These Nights #1201
**In His Sights #1318
**Second-Chance Hero #1351
**Dark Reunion #1452
**Deadly Temptation #1493
**Her Best Friend's
  Husband #1525
Backstreet Hero #1539
Baby's Watch #1544
**His Personal Mission #1573
**The Best Revenge #1597
**Redstone Ever After #1619

Silhouette Desire

Private Reasons #833
Errant Angel #924
A Whole Lot of Love #1281
**Midnight Seduction* #1557

Silhouette Bombshell

Proof #2
Flashback #86

Silhouette Books

*Silhouette Summer
Sizzlers 1994
  "The Raider"
Fortune's Children
The Wrangler's Bride*

*Trinity Street West
**Redstone, Incorporated

JUSTINE DAVIS

lives on Puget Sound in Washington State. Her interests outside writing are sailing, doing needlework, horseback riding and driving her restored 1967 Corvette roadster—top down, of course.

Justine says that years ago, during her career in law enforcement, a young man she worked with encouraged her to try for a promotion to a position that was at the time occupied only by men. "I succeeded, became wrapped up in my new job, and that man moved away, never, I thought, to be heard from again. Ten years later he appeared out of the woods of Washington State, saying he'd never forgotten me and would I please marry him. With that history, how could I write anything but romance?"

When this series began more than nine years ago, the romance world had just lost its staunchest supporter and walking database, *RT Book Reviews* reviewer extraordinaire Melinda Helfer. I still miss her—we are the poorer for her absence. So I'm closing out the REDSTONE, INCORPORATED series the same way I began it, in memory of a guiding light who was one of our best standard-bearers.

Here is a portion of that original dedication.

Once upon a time there was a genre of books that was sadly misunderstood by many people who didn't read them. Those who did read loved them, cherished them, were changed by them. Why? Because they found something in these books that they found nowhere else. Something precious, that spoke to them in a very deep and basic way.

Then one day this beleaguered genre was given a gift. A fairy godmother if you will, a person with an incredible knowledge of these books and why they worked, and an even more incredible generosity of spirit. She was a rock, a pillar on which the genre depended. Her loss has left a gaping hole that can never be filled, and will always be felt by those who love these books—and loved her.

For those reasons and so many more,
the REDSTONE, INCORPORATED series
is dedicated to
MELINDA HELFER

Lost to us August 24, 2000, but if heaven is what it should be she's in an endless library, with an eternity to revel in the books she loved. Happy reading, my friend....

Chapter 1

The man was oblivious.

As Brad Odell talked on, completely unaware, Joshua Redstone watched the deer watch them. A young doe, he thought, frozen as she stared at the intruders, her every muscle tense as she assessed whether to flee. He understood the feeling. He thought of last night, when those coyotes had been yipping around them. The sounds had come from three different directions, giving them the eerie feeling of being triangulated by the wily predators. Josh had spent enough time in places like this, and even wilder places, not to worry, but Odell had seemed edgy. Of course, he'd seemed edgy from the moment they'd started this trek.

Josh had wondered, perhaps uncharitably, if he was nervous at being out of the orbit of his formidable and commanding wife, Diane. The woman was a bit alarming. Some suspected she was the one who really ran things, and Brad was often mute in her presence.

Now he was guessing it was much more than that. If the

man's company hadn't been Redstone's biggest supplier of custom-machined parts, Josh wouldn't be here at all. But Odell, who had invited him several times to explore this piece of California wilderness, had been particularly insistent this time. So he had come, and had—except for his companion's constant chatter—enjoyed the trek.

Or as Tess would call it, the expedition. She always teased him about the condition he came back in, which she laughingly termed as *unrecognizable.* And Josh always countered that it wasn't his fault his beard grew faster than any other man's on the planet, and that after three days he looked as if he hadn't shaved for a week.

Still unaware of the deer's presence, Odell kept walking and talking. Josh amused himself by calculating the doe's comfort zone—at what point the human presence would break that perimeter and send her dashing to safety.

As I should have done, he thought wryly.

Tess had warned him. And the woman who had been friend, ally and confidant for twenty years was rarely wrong.

Just the thought of her made him smile inwardly. He couldn't imagine Redstone—or life—without Tess Machado. She was one of the three who were the foundation of Redstone.

The triumvirate.

John Draven, former special-ops soldier and now legendary head of Redstone Security, Dameron St. John, his right-hand man, and Tess, the woman who could fly anything airworthy and just about anything that wasn't. The three who had been with him virtually from the beginning, the three who were the foundation of what he'd built, the ones who had helped him make Redstone what it was today. Harlan McClaren, the first man to see the potential of Josh's dream and put his money behind it, had coined the moniker, and it had stuck.

He sighed inwardly. Normally, he would have enjoyed being here in this wild place outside Yosemite. They hadn't seen another human being in nearly thirty hours, and to him that wasn't necessarily a bad thing. Which was why he took treks like this regularly.

Too bad Odell talks enough for a dozen people, Josh thought, feeling as if he'd been on this trek with a crowd.

"—regulations made it impossible to do anything with it," Odell was saying. "And I can't afford to just let it sit and pay the taxes on it."

"They'd like that," Josh said, dragging himself back to the present. This, at least, was something he could empathize with. "All this land essentially under their control without having to pay for it? And getting tax revenue from it to boot?"

"They offered to buy it for a nature reserve. Problem is," Odell said, "their idea of 'fair market value' is ridiculous. They might as well just seize it."

"But there's that pesky Fifth Amendment."

"I don't know about that," Odell said.

But you should, Josh thought.

"But I do know I can't afford it." He gave Josh a sideways look. "I need the most I can get for it to keep General Machine afloat."

And there it was, at last. It had taken the man a day and a half to work up to it. It was like Odell to leave it until now, when they were on their way back. Which was probably the crux of all his problems anyway; he never had been good at looking ahead. Josh had figured it was something like this. He'd hoped not, but even his generally optimistic nature hadn't been able to overlook the obvious.

At least, he thought resignedly, it was a beautiful place to have to listen to a sales pitch.

Tess Machado hummed under her breath as she updated her pilot's log, a catchy, bouncy number by a band she'd heard the other day in Samantha Gamble's car. Little Joshua Gamble, the first baby to arrive out of the seemingly continuous swath of new relationships and marriages that had overtaken

Redstone—and the first of likely many, she guessed, to be named after Josh in some way—loved music, and his happy efforts at singing along had been heart-touchingly sweet.

"Lucky boy," she whispered to herself. "You've got a daddy who can make you anything in the world you'd ever want, a mommy who can keep you safer than just about any other and an uncle who loves nothing more than to play with you for hours."

Sam's little brother, Billy—the boy she'd fought so hard to keep with her after their parents were killed and the powers that be insisted a nineteen-year-old girl couldn't take care of a special-needs seven-year-old—adored his baby nephew, and Sam saw to it that they spent as much time together as possible. Thanks to Redstone—and Josh—Billy had his own place in an adult living center now, and had a special area of his main room set apart for little Josh, with toys and books he himself loved.

Finished with her log, Tess wondered if she should start the preflight. She knew only approximately when Josh would arrive; when he took off on these treks the first thing he jettisoned was his watch. Not that it mattered much, he had an internal clock that was almost as accurate as anything he might strap on to his wrist.

She'd leave it for him, she thought. There was, as always after these hikes, a good chance he was going to want to fly. It was his way of making the transition back into the Redstone world, taking the controls of one of the planes that had built it. He hated not being able to fly all the time. She knew it wasn't anything to do with her, but simply that he'd much prefer to be flying himself, as he always had until the burden of the Redstone empire had required him to utilize those hours spent aloft to work.

For a moment she just sat in the cockpit of the Hawk V, the smallest, quickest, most efficient and agile jet in the Redstone fleet. Ryan Barton, Redstone's head computer geek, had once worked up a calculation of how much money was saved by Josh flying the more efficient Redstone planes, how much was gained by him being able to be in full contact and work mode while flying. He'd then factored in all the various attendant costs of flying commercially, stacked it all up versus the jet's comparatively low operating expenses, and the results had been stunning. And the cornerstone of Redstone's admittedly modest advertising budget for some time now.

Not, Tess thought, that they needed to advertise much. The Redstone name did that, simply by existing. The name stood for quality in so many ways, Eric had said.

For the first time in a long time, a rush of memory flooded her, and her eyes teared up. She gave it a moment now, let herself remember her husband's cocky grin, his lean, compact body, that way he'd had of tilting his head just so when he looked at her. She stopped before she could remember how his eyes would heat up as he wondered if he had time to take her back to bed before he headed out to whatever bit of chaos he'd been assigned to fight. She'd always known every time could be the last time. She'd even thought she'd accepted the possibility.

Until it happened. Until her love had come home from a distant war in a flag-draped coffin.

It had been Josh who had gotten her through. He'd stuck to her like glue for six months, never letting her be completely alone, although he left her plenty of space for her grief. He had simply looked at her with those steady gray eyes and said "Trust me. I know how this works."

And it was the knowledge that he did know—with painful intimacy, the path she must now tread—that had let her hand all else over to him, leaving her the monstrous grief to simply endure.

And endure she had, because there had been no other choice. She focused, as Josh instructed, not on what she would do now, not on what her suddenly distant and cold future held, but simply on getting through, not the next day or even hour, but the next minute. And then the next. And one foot after the other, with Josh guiding her, she had finally stepped once more out into the light.

"Enough," she told herself, yanking herself back to the present before the past swamped her.

She glanced at her watch, a complicated pilot's chronometer that nearly dwarfed her small wrist. But it had custom features she loved, including a flight calculator that could factor distance, air speed, fuel consumption, and anticipated weather, so that she could give a fairly accurate flight time for any trip at a moment's notice. She was constantly offered large amounts of cash for it whenever another pilot saw what it could do, and had often told its designer, Redstone's own Ian Gamble, he should mass produce it. Sam's husband always laughed; although Redstone paid him handsomely, he was, she knew, in it for the excitement of making an idea work, not the money.

They were, most thought, an odd couple, Tess mused as she went back into the main cabin. The vibrant, crack security agent and the genius inventor they called, when he got absorbed in an idea to the exclusion of all else, the absent-minded professor. But Sam merely laughed, saying as long as what he got absorbed in was her often enough, she was happy.

A lovely thought, Tess mused as she walked back to the galley—a compact, finely finished space that could handle meals for small groups as well as any kitchen. She put on a fresh pot of coffee, knowing Josh would be wanting it. Then she unlatched the door to the main cabin and lowered the hydraulic steps. Josh had given her a two-hour window, and it was about halfway over, so she expected him shortly.

He'd want to be wheels up as soon as possible, she knew, so she wanted to be sure they were ready. The plane was scheduled for an angel flight this evening, transporting a seriously ill child from a small, central California town just the other side of those mountains, to a pediatric clinic in Los Angeles; it was a cause Josh had long ago dedicated the Hawk fleet to, and he often flew them personally.

She pondered starting the engines now, but decided to wait. It wasn't worth the wasted fuel. One of the many nice things about the little plane, besides the ability to get easily in and out of small airfields like this one, was its quick start-up, which added to its incredible and by now famous efficiency.

She went back to the cockpit. She would adjust the seat and harness now to Josh's settings—being that he was a foot taller than she, it was quite a change—and the copilot's seat to her own. That done, she sat for a moment, looking out toward the mountains thinking about the sort of peace Josh always seemed to find on these expeditions.

"I'll bet you didn't find much with Brad Odell," she mused aloud.

A sound on the gangway steps made her smile.

Finally, she thought. And tried to ignore how much she'd missed him, worried about him, out there in the wilds.

Their relationship was so complicated, their lives so intertwined, and yet separate. Josh had become good friends with Eric, and his own beloved Elizabeth had been like the sister Tess had never had, and each knew the other still grieved, in their way. They rarely spoke of it anymore, but it was still there, and always would be.

All it was, Tess told herself, all it would ever be, was a longtime employee missing a kind, generous boss who had become a friend. She couldn't afford to mess up everything by getting tangled up in emotions she had no business feeling, not about this man.

She got up and opened the cockpit door. "Coffee's fresh, I just put it on," she called out as she stepped back into the cabin.

She stopped dead as two men spun around to face her. Two complete strangers.

One of them smiled, a smile she didn't like at all.

"Well, well, now isn't this nice?" he said, looking her up and down in a way that made her skin crawl.

No, Tess thought. It wasn't nice at all. Because they weren't just strangers. They were also armed.

She knew instantly, deep in her gut, that this was it, that it had finally happened. Everyone at Redstone's worst nightmare had finally come true.

They'd come for Josh.

Chapter 2

Josh was having trouble focusing on Odell's pitch. They had reached the man's expensive German sedan, looking a bit odd parked at the backcountry trailhead, and would soon be headed back toward the airport.

They threw their packs and gear in the trunk. Josh glanced at a young couple setting out on the trail they'd just come back on, then got into the front. He waited, doubting Odell had given up yet. His answer, sadly, was already a given; there was no way he could help the man. So his mind kept wandering. And as it had of late, perhaps reminded by the sight of that happy couple, it kept going down that path he tried to avoid.

He'd once joked that when St. John fell in love, he'd know the world was coming to an end. And apparently he should be preparing, because it had happened. In the most unlikely of ways, but with the most likely, and probably the only woman in the world who thoroughly understood the man who had been a mysterious legend at Redstone for years.

He had no doubts, as he had none about all the other

couples Redstone had brought together, that St. John and his Jessa would make it. There was something about the way his right-hand man looked at her, a trust he never thought he'd see in his wary friend's eyes, that told him this was it, the real thing.

The water, he thought, thinking of the joke that had become a standard line among them. *Maybe it really was the Redstone water.*

It had become such a part of the Redstone lore that it had grown; the word was now you didn't even have to drink it, walking through the fine spray from the waterfall in the Redstone Headquarters was enough.

Rider, he thought. It had all started then, with Noah Rider and Paige. They'd been the first, and the rest had gone down like a string of dominoes, each one seeming, in retrospect, inevitable. As, perhaps, it was. Tess had always said that when you brought together the best—people with the Redstone spirit and way of looking at things—they already had so much in common it was bound to happen.

He had come to think she was right, as usual. He was just having trouble with how it was making him feel.

"I know you saw all this coming," Odell was saying as they sat there in the vehicle, the man making no move to turn the key yet.

For a moment he thought Odell had somehow, bizarrely, read his thoughts. Then he realized he was still on his pitch, and this was his compliment, meant to pump up his ego and make him more amenable.

But Josh Redstone never let his ego get involved in his business. Not that he wasn't certain of himself, he was, but he didn't live on the assumption he was better than anyone else. It mostly turned out he was, but he'd made just enough mistakes about people to keep him humble. So far, the damage done had been minimal or reparable, and he had every intention of keeping it that way.

"I should have listened to you," Odell was saying. "I never should have taken that money, but I didn't see any other way."

"Bankruptcy. Restructuring."

"I couldn't do that. Diane's grandfather built this company. I couldn't be the one to let it fail."

And there was the difference, Josh thought. Odell had let his ego into it, and it had spelled disaster.

"And now Carter is circling."

Josh registered the name. Carter Tool had low bid a Redstone project once but he had turned them down and gone with General instead. That was back when it had been run by Brad's feisty, eighty-three-year-old grandfather-in-law, and had been the best around. He just didn't care for the way Carl Carter did business.

"They know we're ripe for plucking, and they've got the in with the local politicians, they're counting on taking us over to fatten their bottom line."

It was time to put an end to this, before the man started begging. Josh was tough, but not so tough he enjoyed saying no to a man who was groveling.

"I wish I could help, Brad. I truly do. But I can't attach Redstone in any way to a company in the position you're in. They've been looking for a way into Redstone for a long time now, and I can't open even one small door for them."

"But you'd just be buying some land," Odell protested.

"And whose name is it in? Yours or the company's?"

"Well, the company, but—"

Josh held up a hand. "That's all they'd need. The Redstone name on any transaction with a company they've taken over. That's how they do it."

"They haven't taken over yet."

"Brad," Josh said sadly, "they took over the day you cashed their check."

"I had no choice," the man said dully, clearly realizing now that Josh meant what he said.

That's what they wanted you to think.

Josh didn't say it aloud. Just as he didn't let his ego get in his way, he also didn't believe in kicking a man when he was down.

"I wish I could help. If you'd come to me before…"

He let his words trail off, seeing no point in rubbing salt in the wound. Because if Brad *had* come to him then, he would have done what he could to prop up the ailing manufacturer who had supplied several of the parts used in Redstone engines.

Odell sighed, heavily. He took out his cell phone, checked for a signal, sent a quick text message. And then, finally, he started the car and they headed down to the flats. In silence.

The silence held for the entire ninety-minute drive down the narrow mountain road. Josh felt regret, but turned his mind to other things. Finally, they reached the turnoff to the small airport. Josh immediately spotted the Hawk V, ready and waiting, the trademark red-and-gray paint job gleaming quietly in the sun. It never failed to give him a kick of pride to see it, this latest in the line, that was breaking efficiency records all over the country, without sacrificing speed or comfort.

Bless you, Ian, he thought in silent tribute to the man whose lightweight and impossibly strong composite had made it possible. Ian's explanation of the nanotechnology involved—which included a reference to Buckminster Fuller—had made his eyes glaze, but seeing the result made his heart race.

He got out of the car, and grabbed his pack from the trunk. Then he turned to look at Odell, who hadn't even gotten out of the driver's seat. He sat, staring at the Hawk V, an odd expression on his face. Regret, sadness and something else Josh couldn't put a name to.

"I'm sorry, Brad," Josh said softly. "I mean that."

"I know you do," the dejected man said.

There was nothing more to say, really, so Josh left it at that. And after a moment of awkward silence, Odell drove away, his cell phone already in his hand again.

Josh slung the small pack—he made do with very little for such a short trek—over one shoulder, and rubbed at the back of his neck. For the first time in a long time, he was simply, purely tired, and it had nothing to do with the four-hour tramp into the backcountry and back out again. This was a mental weariness he'd never felt before, the exhaustion of spending far too much time dodging the kind of figurative bullet that had taken General Machine down, and far too little doing what he loved, guiding Redstone. Thanks to diversification, determination and, he admitted, his own stubbornly independent streak, Redstone was strong and solid. The endless work and sweat and drive of the Redstone family had made it what it was around the world, and was keeping it that way. But at a price.

He strode across the tarmac toward the waiting plane, his spirits picking up a bit. Tess would cheer him up. Her lovely face would light up, as it always did, at the sight of him, giving him the lift that could only come from someone you liked and respected being so glad to see you.

Ego definitely involved there, he thought with an inward grin.

The backpack was sufficiently grubby that he paused to toss it in the cargo hold of the Hawk before he started up the steps that were down and waiting. He should have called the moment they were in the car, he thought. Then Tess could have had it warmed up and ready to go. But it hadn't seemed right to show that his focus was on getting back to his own business when he was listening to the death knell of someone else's.

He closed the hatch to the cargo hold, knowing Tess would

hear the sound and know he was there. In fact, he half expected to hear the jet fire up before he reached the stairs, and when it didn't, figured she must be in the middle of something else. Idle time was a rarity with Tess; about the only time she ever sat still was to read.

He could afford, he thought, to take the controls for the angel flight. Time enough to get to work when they were back in Southern California. That was encouragement enough to have him trotting up the steps into the cabin, already anticipating the adrenaline surge as they lifted off. That was one thing that never failed him, the joy he felt at the controls of a responsive, quick, well-built airplane.

At the top of the steps, as he stepped into the plane, he called out for Tess.

"Hey, Machado, you goofing off? Better watch it, I hear your boss is on his way back."

He frequently teased her with that, since it was so far from the truth at any given moment. Not to mention he never felt like he was her boss, anyway. She wasn't his employee, she was Tess.

Three things happened the moment he put a booted foot down in the main cabin.

He saw two men, strangers, one on each side of the doorway, both of them with their right hands beneath lightweight jackets. And he saw Tess across the cabin, standing facing the doorway, her arms crossed, her slender fingers gripping her elbows as if to hold herself together. Her expression was tight, her usually golden complexion pale.

Something was very wrong.

The third thing was the explanation he dreaded, but already half expected, even in the split second he'd had to process what was happening.

"Hello, Michael," Tess said, her voice as tight as her expression.

Michael.

His middle name. Used by no one, not even him. Not because he hated it, not because there was no need, since there was little likelihood of him being confused with another Joshua Redstone, if there even was one. But unused because it was reserved for a specific situation, by order of John Draven, the legendary head of the equally legendary Redstone Security team.

Reserved for one single instance that Josh had reluctantly had to admit to his sternly fatalistic security chief was a real possibility.

Reserved as warning, as explanation, as trigger.

Reserved for a hostage situation.

And Tess had just let him know the grim truth. He was the hostage.

It had finally happened.

Chapter 3

For a moment, Tess didn't dare breathe. Let alone speak. And not because they'd threatened her if she gave them away. She didn't even think about that. She knew Josh would get the message of her use of his middle name. But he had no way of knowing what else she'd learned in the few minutes she'd had with these thugs before he'd gotten here.

It was only chance, good fortune, that the teasing greeting he so often tossed out to her played right into that knowledge and the ignorance she'd discovered. As did his scruffy, unkempt appearance after his mountain trek, just as she'd hoped.

She watched his steady gray eyes as he looked at the two men. She could almost feel his agile brain firing, assessing, and knew he was calculating the possibility of success if he put a halt to this right now. But Josh was no fool, she knew he had to realize they were armed.

The two men, on the other hand, seemed incredibly slow on the uptake, simply staring at the newcomer.

"These guys just got here," she said, knowing some explanation was called for if they were to pull this off. She'd had a few minutes to think, to plan, to come up with a story. "They're guards. There have been some threats."

She saw his eyes narrow slightly, and tried to think how to let him know what the situation truly was.

"It's serious. They're armed. I don't know if there's going to be time for you to make that repair, Michael," she added, trying to keep her voice even as she repeated the code name. "Mr. Redstone is due back any minute."

The pause before he spoke was so slight Tess doubted anyone but herself would really notice. "Running late, is he?"

Tess breathed again as he picked up her clue. "You know how he is."

"Yes," Josh said. "I do."

One of the armed men snorted. "Figures. Big shots always think nobody's time matters but theirs."

"Shut up," the other man snapped, apparently realizing it wasn't an appropriate reaction if they were actually here to protect Josh. The fact that he seemed willing to go along with the fiction she'd presented gave her hope; maybe Josh could actually turn around and walk right out of here, and they wouldn't know they actually had had, and lost, their quarry.

It was a possibility she'd latched on to the moment she'd realized there was a good chance they wouldn't recognize him, not fresh out of the woods, unshaven and in worn clothes and a pair of hiking boots that had seen many miles. The moment she'd realized they hadn't even recognized Josh in the single photograph that was here in the main cabin, a shot of Josh and herself with the manager of the small airport where this very Hawk V had first strutted her stuff.

When they'd noticed the picture, they had assumed the perfectly groomed man in the suit, not the man casually dressed in a beyond battered bomber jacket and cowboy boots, was the head of the vaunted Redstone empire. And while there was a slight resemblance in height and leanness, Tess knew the mistake was only possible because no static image could ever capture the dynamic power and force that hid behind the laid-back personality of the real Joshua Redstone.

They, or whoever had hired them, hadn't done their homework, or were incapable of making the jump from their perceptions to reality. That gave her another clue as to the kind of men these were. Sloppy. Or stupid. And that could be both helpful and dangerous.

The armed man who had belatedly taken charge turned back to look at Josh. "You some kind of mechanic?"

"Something like that," Josh said, shifting his gaze. There was, Tess noticed, barely a trace of his usual easy drawl. It had been there when he'd called out his greeting, but she hoped the men would think he was just imitating her boss, the man his very words had indicated wasn't here yet.

"What's wrong with this fancy plane?"

Again there was the barest of hesitations, and Tess knew Josh was thinking fast. "Problem with the electrical system," he said.

Perfect, she thought. That would keep them on the ground. Too many lethal possibilities in the air.

"Guess you have to go get your tools?" she suggested.

Go. Get clear, get safe.

The words echoed in her mind like some fierce chant, as if she could will him to do it by sheer silent force of will.

"I don't think so," Josh said slowly. "Now that I'm here, I'm not about to leave."

She heard his subtext as clearly as if he'd spoken it; no way would Josh leave one of his own in jeopardy to save his own skin. Tess smothered a sigh; it had been worth a try, even though she'd known he wouldn't take the chance for escape, not if it meant leaving her here. Not even to call in the cavalry.

No more than she would leave him to save herself.

Not that she was any more special to him than anyone from Redstone. Well, maybe a little more, she conceded at the gentle rebuke in his eyes at her attempt.

"There are tools here on the plane," he said. "Might as well use them."

Did he mean the weapons? Tess wondered.

"Just do it fast," one of the men, the tall, almost cadaverous one in the brown shirt snapped.

Josh didn't even flinch. "This plane's got miles of wiring. It's going to take a while to isolate the problem."

"Mr. Redstone's not going to like that," Tess said, trying to imagine what the response would be for an employee a little afraid of a nasty boss.

"Tough," Josh said, with a one-shouldered shrug. "This plane doesn't leave until I clear it."

The brown shirt snorted, clearly amused by the thought of a mere mechanic ordering around Josh Redstone. Tess kept her eyes on Josh, hoping he'd see what she saw, something to be used.

"Maybe you shouldn't start until he's here, and explain to him. You know how he is."

"Afraid he'll take it out on you, honey?" the smaller of the armed men said, with a shockingly genuine-sounding note of commiseration in his voice. He wore an unintentionally colored shirt; it appeared to have originally been white, with a familiar environmental slogan on the front, but it now had the pinkish cast of something whitewashed with something new and red.

Pinky, she thought. That's the kind of nickname he deserved. Pinky and Brown Shirt, perfect for the morons they were.

"Knock it off, Romeo," Brown Shirt snapped.

"Hey," Pinky countered, "chances are she could be on our side." *Our side?* Tess wondered.

"She's stuck working for the bastard."

"I believe," she said, affecting a disinterested tone, "Mr. Redstone's parents were married long before he was born."

Pinky looked blank. "Huh?"

Brown Shirt rolled his eyes. Tess noted the impatience in both his voice and body language; if there was already trouble in the ranks, perhaps they could use that, too. She flicked a quick glance at Josh. Those intense gray eyes, always at odds with his laid-back, sometimes even lazy seeming demeanor, were sharply focused, and she knew his prodigious mind was racing even faster than her own.

"Just fix the damned thing, and fast," Brown Shirt said to Josh. His gaze flicked briefly to Tess. "Don't want big man Redstone taking it out on us little guys."

"So you've been working for him for a while?" Josh asked, hitting just the right note of casual query.

"Don't have to to know they're all alike, those big CEO's. Now get to it, will you?"

Tess frowned inwardly. What was this, some kind of protest mounted by idiots too blind to honestly find out who they were targeting? Didn't they realize they were dealing with a man who would—and had—send the troops out for the lowliest employee just as quickly as for one of his executives? She had assumed money was the goal, but now—

"Heard any system alarms go off?"

Josh's question was aimed at her, and she yanked herself out of ponderings there was no time for now. Motivation didn't matter at the moment, the reality of the situation did.

Josh was barely a foot away now. She saw his gaze flick for a split second to the armed men. "Pinky and Brown Shirt," she muttered, so lowly only he could hear. She saw one corner of his mouth lift for another fraction of a second as he registered the insulting nicknames.

"Not yet," she answered in a calm, normal tone, as if he really were that mechanic, and understanding he'd really been asking if she'd been able to set off the duress alarms yet. Another Draven insistence. Although the best method was the computer hookup, where more details could be sent. There were also triggers in the cockpit, the main stateroom and especially the head; almost anyone taken hostage, Draven had explained, could convince their captors they needed to use the head.

Of course, if Draven had his way, there would be Redstone Security on every flight his boss took. And for the first time Tess, who had always treasured flight time alone with Josh, wished the man had acceded to his security chief's request.

"You got the computer on?" Josh asked.

"Not yet," Tess answered again.

"Computer?" Brown Shirt frowned. "What do you need the computer for?"

"Diagnostics," Josh said blandly. "Have to find out where the problem is."

"Do it without."

"Impossible. That's where the schematics are."

"The what?" asked Pinky.

Brown Shirt ignored him. "Bull. What did they do before computers?"

"Before computers, electrical systems were much simpler," Josh said. "Even on airplanes." Then, with a perfect rendition of a merely puzzled man and a glance at Tess, he asked, "What's the problem? Is the system down?"

"Redstone doesn't want anyone going online from here," Brown Shirt answered.

Josh didn't turn a shaggy hair at the disrespect in the man's words and tone.

"I don't need to go online. The schematics are right there on the onboard computer."

Tess wondered if he was having trouble keeping the drawl out of his voice. It was pointed out in every article that had ever been written about him, it seemed, mentioning how it often lulled people into thinking he was slow or stupid, that he had somehow stumbled into his good fortune and wealth, or acquired it on the backs of others. But people who made those assumptions soon learned that they had sadly underestimated him on all counts. Usually too late. And even these apparently uninformed assailants might put it together if they heard that drawl.

Fortunately, those articles almost always used the formal portrait of a clean-cut Josh that he had reluctantly sat for several years ago. He'd sworn he would never do it again, saying that people were one day going to be surprised when they met him and found out he was ninety-five, because he'd still be using that portrait. The portrait he looked nothing like right now, not with his bearded jaw and shaggy, tousled hair. But then, he'd always said, "We're selling Redstone value, not me."

Brown Shirt looked as if he were having a terrible time making a decision. Tess wasn't sure if that was good for them or not.

"Besides," Josh said after a moment of studying Brown Shirt's expression, "I don't work for Redstone, anyway. He can't order me around like he does everyone else."

"That's Mr. Redstone to you," Tess said, struck with a sudden inspiration. And again Josh got her intent instantly.

"Yeah, yeah," he said, as if bored with it all. "I know, he's the big wheel. Big deal."

Brown Shirt smiled. And decided. "You do the computer," he said, gesturing at Josh. "And you," he said to Tess, in a much different tone, "back off. Don't even get near it."

Josh shrugged as if he hadn't noticed the change at all. As if their attitude toward her was to be expected. He walked toward the glossy rosewood desk that held the sleek-looking computer setup.

"Hey!" Pinky, who had been quiet for a while, broke his silence. "Hey, he's the guy in the photo!"

Tess's breath caught. Her mind raced, figuring they had only seconds to deal with this.

"What?" Brown Shirt wheeled to look at his partner.

"He's the guy in the picture," Pinky said, pointing at the frame fastened to the wall over the desk.

Josh glanced up at the picture, shrugging as if he'd seen it a hundred times. As, indeed, he had. "Yeah," he said, tone absent, unimpressed as he turned back to the computer. "That was the maiden flight of this bird. Guess he didn't have much faith in it, wanted a mechanic along."

He'd hit just the right note of indifference and matched Brown Shirt's own undertone of disrespect; Tess saw it register on Brown Shirt's face. She didn't dare look at Josh as they waited to see if it was all going to fall apart here and now.

Brown Shirt studied the picture for a long, silent moment. Josh looked as if he were thinking of saying more; she hoped he wouldn't, because "Michael" wouldn't.

Even as she thought it, he clearly reached the same conclusion, because he glanced at her and threw out a diversion instead.

"Boss is really on a rampage, huh?"

Tess recovered quickly, relieved. She shrugged. "He gets that way. You know how it is. You don't expect somebody in his position to be kind, generous or go way beyond the call for his people."

All of which Josh was and did, and if these clowns had done their homework they'd have known that. And for just an instant as he looked at her, she saw acknowledgment of the compliment she'd just indirectly paid him. Not that it wasn't anything she hadn't said to him directly before; he knew quite well she thought the world of him.

He just didn't know she was in love with him, and had been for a very long time.

Chapter 4

Josh was in a difficult place. He'd put together his crack security team to protect Redstone around the world, and to help any Redstone employee who needed it. And led by Draven they'd done a stellar job, all of them. They were ever ready to mobilize at a moment's notice.

He'd just never wanted to have to mobilize them for himself.

He sat there, studying the complex wiring diagram as if he were truly seeking the nonexistent electrical problem. He hadn't yet keyed in the signal that would do just that—mobilize Redstone Security. Once he did, unless that signal was canceled within five minutes, that was it, there would be no calling them off. John Draven wouldn't stop until it was over, and over his way.

But it was what might happen in between that bothered Josh. He'd heard often enough from his people that they'd walk through fire for him. The declarations always made him uncomfortable; he didn't see himself as they did, and his answer was usually something awkward like "Just give me your best work." That's the principle Redstone was built on; hire the best, then get out of their way. He'd always believed in it. And that included, perhaps most especially, Redstone Security. And they were the best. Draven had done the near-impossible, built a private security force that had the respect and cooperation of their public counterparts around the world.

But he didn't want them, or anyone, risking themselves for him. And if he sent that duress code, that was inevitably going to happen.

He hit a few keys that did nothing, then the one that paged the diagram downward; he wanted them used to him occasionally typing. The more information he could send in that signal, the better.

If he sent it at all.

"Get us some food," Brown Shirt—the perfect name for him, Josh had thought when Tess had whispered it—suddenly ordered with a gesture at her. A gesture that parted his jacket enough for Josh to see the blocky, bulky pistol jammed in his waistband. Not a holster, like a pro.

"Excuse me?" Tess said, as if she hadn't heard him right.

"Food," he repeated. "It's what you do, isn't it, serve passengers? This fancy plane must have food."

A realization belatedly clicked into place for him. They had no idea they were talking to the pilot of this plane. That, he thought, smothering the unexpected urge to smile, would cost them.

"Why, of course," Tess said sweetly. Too sweetly. "What can I get you? Caviar? Pâté?"

Pinky snorted. And again Josh had to fight a smile; fish eggs and liver had never been high on his list of what to stock on the Redstone fleet. But he also wished Tess would stop baiting them; the bottom line was still that they were armed and he—for the moment at least—was not.

That gave him pause. Tess was the smartest, quickest person he'd ever known, even St. John took longer than she did to assess a situation. But she had the razor-sharp quickness of a good pilot who dealt with rapidly changing conditions on a regular basis. And she also never spoke carelessly or heedlessly.

Which meant she'd chosen her words specifically, with purpose.

To confirm they had no idea who they had here? To show him they were, for all their blustering, totally unprepared at best, or inept at worst?

Josh smothered a grimace. If there was anything worse than inept, unprepared people with guns, he couldn't think offhand what it was.

And he knew he would send that code. Because it wasn't just him here. It was Tess. She'd been through too much pain in life already. She deserved the best possible chance to get out of this unscathed. That meant they needed the best possible help.

And that meant Redstone Security.

"And pull up those steps until your boss gets here," Brown Shirt added as Tess continued to stare at him. "No sense allowing anybody else to stumble in here."

And realizing you're here, Josh thought.

Tess did as ordered, then moved toward the galley, as if she really were that flight attendant they apparently thought her. That was something he'd never gone for, either; if you were on board a Redstone plane at all, you knew where the food was and were at home enough to get it yourself. There was the occasional business-meeting flight where someone would take over the prep chores, but it was as likely to be he himself as anyone else.

Brown Shirt was hovering, looking at the complex schematic on the screen. Josh typed again, the useless combo, then the page down key.

"You understand that crap?"

Actually, he did. He'd designed the plane, after all. "It's my job," he said.

A little too sharp there, Redstone, he thought. So he adopted a friendly tone that would have been appropriate if they really had been Redstone people and he the private mechanic.

"Lot of wiring, even on a plane this small."

"It is small," Brown Shirt agreed. "I would have thought a big shot like Redstone would use a bigger one."

That was it, he thought. That was what Tess had wanted to tell him. That these men were working on perceptions, not reality. They had expectations, stereotypical ones, about the head of an enterprise the size of Redstone. And he wasn't meeting them.

"Efficiency," Josh said as he went through the fake sequence again, as if it took a dozen keystrokes instead of one to simply page down in the complicated diagram. "Square cube law."

"Square what?"

"Square cube law," Josh said absently, as if he were engrossed in the diagram. "Double the size of a plane, you quadruple its weight."

"Huh?" Brown Shirt grunted.

"Weight's important." He made his voice as much of a drone as he could. "The wings need a specific air speed to make enough lift, and a heavier airplane takes longer to get to that speed. And more runway, so you're limited to fields that can handle that. Then when you're airborne, a heavier plane flies slower than a lighter one at the same power, so if you want to maintain the same speed, it takes more power, and thus fuel."

"Yeah, right," Brown Shirt muttered, clearly, and just as Josh had hoped, bored.

"Then of course there's landing with a heavy airplane. Kinetic energy and all. Mass is mass, and that plane only stops when you—"

"I get it," Brown Shirt said, backing away before Josh could inundate him with more. Josh doubted he did, in fact, get it, but he didn't care as long as the man's attention was turned elsewhere.

The moment the man's attention was on Tess coming back with something on a tray, he hit the unique button that activated the direct connection to security. Then he typed in the real sequence Draven had developed long ago. Signed it with his middle name. He didn't have to send it; it had gone live from the moment he'd activated the direct link.

He noted the time on his battered yet still accurate aviator's watch he'd strapped on after the trek. It had been given to him all those years ago by Mac McClaren on the occasion of the first flight of the Hawk I. Seeing that Brown Shirt was still focused on the sandwiches Tess had brought, he activated the elapsed time feature. Then he went back to the diagram, thinking he would stall until they started to get suspicious.

That, unfortunately, didn't take long.

"What are you doing? What's taking so long?" Pinky asked, a slightly whiny note in his voice as he spoke around a mouthful of ham sandwich. He gulped down a swallow of the bottled water he held in his other hand as he hovered over Josh, peering at the screen. With the movement, Josh caught a glimpse of a semiautomatic pistol digging into the man's too generous belly, confirming his guess that they were both armed.

"Verifying," Josh said. "Wouldn't want to cut the wrong wire and have your altimeter not work."

Pinky's face scrunched up slightly. "What's an altim—what you said do?"

"Tells you how high you are so you don't slam into the side of one of these mountains."

The man paled slightly. Swallowed. "Oh."

Pinky retreated, apparently not liking being reminded of the grim possibilities of flight. Josh wondered if they planned on letting them get airborne. Or maybe the plan was that this whole thing was to be conducted on the ground.

Or maybe they didn't really have a plan at all.

Josh sneaked a look at his watch; less than a minute and a half to go now. Brown Shirt glanced his way, as if checking his progress.

He decided he'd pushed his luck as far as he could just now. He hit the keys that would blank out the screen, as if he'd shut down the system. A couple of small LED lights still glowed, but he hoped they either wouldn't notice, or wouldn't realize it meant the system was still on. The screen would only reactivate at the proper command, from here or from Redstone Security, not simply the touch of a key.

But the webcams and microphones would still be live.

Josh pushed the keyboard back into its cubby, bumping the edge of the monitor as if by accident in the process, turning it slightly more toward the main cabin. It would help if they had a wider view. There were three other cams on the plane, and they could all be accessed from outside by security. Draven was nothing if not thorough.

It was as he made that move that he noticed a magazine that had slid to the floor between the desk and the side of the plane. Automatically, he reached toward it to pick it up.

Tess coughed. He glanced at her. Caught the briefest flick of her eyes. And stopped, abruptly remembering that it was likely the business magazine she'd brought on board on the flight up here, to show him the article that had just been done on the breadth of Redstone's Research and Development division. The quick-thinking Tess had likely made sure that magazine had vanished; his picture, that formal head shot, had been on the cover. And even though he looked little like it now, Tess had obviously decided not to tempt fate.

Which left only the photograph on the opposite bulkhead. But for safety it was bolted to the wall, so there wasn't much to be done about that one. And it appeared they'd believed Tess's clever feint, and thought him simply a mechanic Redstone had hired both in that picture and here and now.

He stood up. Brown Shirt wheeled around, half a sandwich in his left hand, his right still free for his weapon. So he wasn't completely stupid, Josh thought.

"Looks like the problem's in the cockpit. I'll need to open up the floor in there."

Brown Shirt frowned. "How long is this going to take?"

"Won't know until I get in there. You in a hurry?" He used the comment as excuse to glance at his watch.

"Redstone will be. You know those CEO types."

"Yeah," Josh said. The seconds rolled by. Josh adopted an expression of concentration as he watched the time tick by, as if he were truly trying to come up with the answer to Brown Shirt's question.

Five minutes.

It was done. There was no stopping it now.

Chapter 5

"*H, G,* two, two, two, zero, question mark," Samantha Gamble read aloud to those who couldn't see the H/G/2/2/2/0/? string on the computer screen, her voice tight.

Draven knew he didn't have to explain to the five other people in the room. Not even recent addition to the Redstone Security team Logan Beck; Draven made it his business to personally instruct everyone he hired in this, what he considered their most important function. Not that his boss would agree; for Josh, his people took priority over everything else—property, assets…and himself.

"We're sure this is from Josh's plane?" Beck asked.

Draven explained the complex sig line that verified the transmission was indeed from the computer aboard Josh's Hawk V. Then he held the ex-cop's gaze and waited. Beck understood, and quickly translated, showing he'd forgotten nothing of this most emphasized lesson.

"*H* for hostage situation," Beck said. "*G* means they're

still on the ground. The number-slash sequence means two hostages, two perps, two visible weapons and no injuries."

Yet.

The unuttered word echoed in the Redstone Security squad room in the county airport hangar that had housed them for some time now. Draven read in all their faces that they'd heard that word as clearly as they were hearing the bustling sounds of the Redstone ground crew outside. The crew was readying the team's Hawk III, unmarked except for the required tail number and sans the too-well-known Redstone paint job, for flight.

"Question mark," Tony Alvera said, his face set in grim lines as he ran a finger over the distinctive patch of beard below his lower lip. A brightly new wedding band glinted on his ring finger, smooth and simple in contrast to his rather dangerous appearance.

"Motive unknown," Beck said. He was sporting a textured wedding ring that was almost as new. Odd, Draven thought in a moment of digression he once wouldn't have allowed himself, that he himself had been married longer than two of his own. He who had once figured he was destined for a solitary life. He who now had Grace, in all meanings of the name and the word.

And was happier than he'd ever thought possible.

Draven's gaze flicked to the silent, dark man who stood off to one side. When he'd seen St. John's Jessa with a uniquely carved engagement ring on her finger, he'd had to believe anything was possible.

"So they haven't mentioned ransom," Reeve Westin said, almost under her breath, defining aloud what they all knew the question mark in that position in the string meant.

"Only a fool would try that," Sam said. "Josh has made it public knowledge for years that that is his strictest order. No ransom, under any circumstances."

Reeve nodded. "I know. Sadly the world is full of fools, blindness and just plain evil."

Draven knew that no one knew that better than Reeve. Her daily work was full of it. While on liaison to her husband's Westin Foundation, funded in large part by Redstone and specializing in finding missing children, Reeve was still officially Redstone Security. When he and Sam, who were already here, had put the call out, she'd been the last one to arrive. Tony, at lunch with his wife at Redstone Headquarters, had been barely ahead of her.

And St. John had been first. He wasn't Redstone Security, but no one was about to deny him access. Even if not for his intimidating demeanor, he was Josh's right hand, and knew as much if not more of the inner, outer, and every other working of Redstone as Josh himself did. And formally trained or not, Draven would back St. John in just about any fight that came along; he'd grown up hard and tough and smart.

And Josh had always said that if anything happened to him, St. John was the one who could step in and Redstone would never miss a beat.

But nothing, Draven thought with near-violent determination, was going to happen to Josh. He would come through this without a scratch on him. He hadn't built this incredible team to have it fail at the most important mission they'd ever faced. They would succeed, no matter what. And the time for musing about anything other than that goal was over.

"Tess," St. John said.

"Yes," Draven said, acknowledging the likely identity of the second hostage. The grim faces around him turned even grimmer. Draven understood. Tess was an institution at Redstone, a legend. And she'd helped every person in this room at one time or another. Including he himself. Tess was one of the few people outside his own security team who had his complete and total trust and respect. She was the best, coolest fixed wing pilot he'd ever seen, and as good or better in a helicopter. She'd been with Josh even longer than he had, had flown Redstone teams in and out of some of the most difficult spots on the planet, under sometimes even more difficult conditions. Like under fire.

Everybody in this room knew what she meant to Redstone. To each of them.

And to Josh.

"What's the time element now?" Beck asked.

"Based on the computer's mark, seven minutes, thirteen seconds," Draven answered.

He knew he didn't have to explain that, either. The five-minute deadline had passed, and nothing, no e-mail with a cancellation code, no text message or even phone call could stop the full mobilization of Redstone Security now.

"Synch now?" Samantha asked.

Draven nodded, and six wrists raised, including his own, as they set their ultra-accurate chronometers for the next full minute and listened to Sam count down. They were likely all on the same second anyway, the watches being a highly reliable Gamble design, but Redstone Security hadn't become what they were by making assumptions. And what they were was the finest, most successful and respected—even in law enforcement and military circles—private security operation in the world, dedicated to one cause, keeping Redstone and its people safe.

On the minute Sam called the mark in a firm, steady voice, and the six of them started their mission clocks simultaneously.

And Draven began to give his orders. "The crew's got most of the routine gear loaded. Beck, you and Alvera load up the weapons and ammunition." No one but Redstone Security handled their firepower.

"The black box?"

The question came from Reeve, who in fact was the first

agent Draven had hired once Redstone had grown beyond even his immense abilities to cover.

"Yes," Draven said, his tone betraying a tension he knew it was pointless to try to hide, because they would all be feeling it. This was the day they'd all feared, the day they'd all hoped would never come. "Everything goes. I don't want any delays while we wait for gear. This is Josh."

No one commented. They all knew that black box, actually a very large locker, held an assortment of what they jokingly— when nothing was at stake—called odds and ends. Some were simple, almost commonplace, hand grenades and other garden-variety explosives. Some were more exotic, RPG's and a couple of other things that would have likely been frowned upon if owned by any private entity with a lesser reputation than Redstone.

And a couple of things in that box weren't known about at all in the outside world. The genius of Ian Gamble, Redstone's resident inventor and Sam's husband, sometimes ran in some interesting channels.

"Rand is on his way from Seattle. He'll meet us there. Hill is going to be our liaison from here to Redstone Headquarters," Draven said, gesturing to Taylor Hill, the young woman who was the newest member of the vaunted Redstone Security team. It wasn't that he didn't trust her, she wouldn't have made it on to the team if he hadn't had complete faith in her abilities, it was simply that the rest of them had worked together long enough to have become a smooth, precision team.

"Lilith and Liana are setting up the communications center there," Alvera said, referring to his and his sometimes partner Beck's wives respectively. "That way we can all be in the field."

Draven nodded. He'd already okayed giving the two women the codes to directly connect to the security team's computer system; this was war, and if he had to use all of Redstone to save Josh, he would.

"Ryan Barton is on his way," Draven said, "in case we need tech help. We'll lift off as soon as he gets here."

The head of the Redstone ground crew, a young man in gray coveralls and the name "Tim" stitched over the pocket, stuck his head in the door. He looked a little startled, likely because when Draven had first ordered the team plane readied, he and Sam had been the only ones here.

"She's ready, sir," Tim said to Draven. "And you'll have a five-minute takeoff window in ten minutes."

Draven nodded. The county airport was fairly busy, but when Redstone called and said they needed a takeoff slot *now*, they got it. They were the highest-paying private tenant the airport had, because they paid for hangar space for a large part of the Redstone fleet, plus this semi-isolated building on the remotest part of the airfield. Not to mention that Redstone had helped fund the resurfacing of a second runway that had greatly raised the airport's efficiency rating.

And it didn't hurt that they'd only asked for the priority ranking three times in all these years; once when they'd been on their way to rescue one of their own, and twice for an emergency angel flight for a child awaiting a life-saving transplant.

A bright blue PT Cruiser careened around a corner and barked to a halt outside the door. Through the window they saw a young man with rather spiky, blond-tipped hair call out to Tim as he settled a large backpack on his shoulder. The brilliant, self-described tech-head had his own weapons, Draven thought. He watched as Barton headed for the plane rather than the hangar; the sense of urgency had clearly infused them all.

"Suit up," Draven said shortly. "It's time."

There was a rush of movement as the people in the room picked up their gear bags. Sam got to her feet, turning the computer station over to Taylor. The young woman nodded;

if she felt any trepidation at this trial by fire less than a year after getting the coveted spot on the team, it didn't show.

"Sam," Draven began, the faintest of frowns creasing his brow.

The tall, leggy blonde turned to him as if she'd been waiting for this.

"Don't even think about it, John," she said softly, her unusual use of his first name a warning as much as anything. "Ian understands what we both owe Josh, and that there is no way in absolute hell I'm staying behind."

"The baby," he said.

"Ian has him. And if we need Ian, he'll take him to Ryan's mom's."

Draven studied the woman who had become one of his best agents after Josh had plucked her out of the Redstone Security staff at the Sitka resort. Sam never wavered under that gaze he'd been told could bring enemies to their knees. Her voice was steady, cool and unruffled.

"You going to tell Reeve not to come, because she's already taken a bullet for Josh? Or Beck, because he's already nearly died once in a hostage situation? Don't try to make me into someone I'm not. That's not the example I want for my son."

And that, Draven thought, was an argument he couldn't counter. Time was wasting, that takeoff window was nearing, and when it came down to it, he wanted Sam there. Her skill with weapons, her ability to think on her feet and her gorgeous blond presence gave him a flexibility in planning he wanted. More than once it had tipped the scales. Just as, when circumstances were different and required a different sort of approach, Reeve's delicate, fragile look was advantageous. And that look hid a steely strength honed in fire, a strength that had pulled her through when, on one of the few times when the circumstances had warranted even Josh admitting a bodyguard would be wise, she had indeed taken a bullet meant for him.

Both women were highly trained, more than competent, and self-secure enough to use those looks when it helped get the job done, counting it their adversary's problem if they couldn't see past a pretty face.

"All right," he said abruptly. "Let's roll."

Exactly four minutes and thirty-two seconds later they were airborne, and headed for a small airport in the Sierra Nevada mountains.

And they wouldn't leave until the two people they all respected, admired and loved were safe.

Chapter 6

Tess fussed in the galley as if nothing were more important than cleaning up after that impromptu meal. She could keep an eye on Josh from there, and she wanted him in her sights at all times.

He was kneeling beside the hole he'd made by removing a section of the cockpit floor. The mass of wiring was clearly visible, and more than a little daunting. What wasn't visible was the small box fastened to the underside, with a fingerprint-scanning lock openable only by a select few.

Josh was studying the wiring, putting on a more-than-believable show of searching for the nonexistent problem. But Brown Shirt was hovering too close for Josh to go for the small, loaded pistol that was secreted in that box.

She knew quite well that Josh had been aware, ever since he was the most touted wunderkind on the block, that he was a target. His skyrocket success, the rapid ascent as he built the Redstone empire, as he gathered around him those of like mind and brilliance, had brought him to the attention of the country, then the world. And to the attention of those who sought an easy way, not willing to put in the kind of effort and work he did, who had more than once thought to use him as a shortcut to their own wealth.

She also knew that he knew—Draven harped on it enough—that his independent streak put him at greater risk. Only by pointing out that that streak was what got him and Redstone where they were in the first place, had he nudged his chief of security into grudging acceptance that he wasn't going to live with a bodyguard in his pocket 24/7, as Draven would prefer.

Once he'd realized he had to accept that fact, the determined but adaptable Draven had taken another course; he'd made certain that everyone around Josh had some serious training.

Tess fussed with the debris of the hastily prepared sandwiches, purposefully dropping things or knocking things over, going as slowly as possible.

I'd never hire me as a flight attendant, she thought, but thankfully these two didn't seem to notice her fumbling inefficiency that caused as much work as it accomplished.

But then, most men would never have hired me as a pilot, either, not as green as I was.

But Josh had. She'd been hardly more than a kid then, the ink barely dry on her pilot's license, and too few hours in her log. But Josh happened to have been at the airport where she'd set down a small Cessna with a collapsed nose gear in a fierce crosswind that had made it beyond difficult. But she'd done it, and been met at the tie-down by an intense-eyed young man with long, dark hair, who offered her a job with little pay, long hours and all the flight time she wanted.

She'd been doubtful at first; he certainly didn't look like much with those battered boots and worn jeans. Or sound like much, with that drawl that could be Texas, could be New Orleans, or any combination of other places. But the moment he'd shown her his first design, the drawings that had become the Hawk I, she'd jumped at the chance, sensing in some way she'd never quite understood that this man was going places.

And within a decade, Redstone was a name known across the country. Within a half decade more, it was known around the world.

When Josh had eventually accepted—grudgingly—the need for a pilot so he could work on business trips, she'd been pleased that of all the pilots he now had working for Redstone, it was her he came to.

And the day after she'd accepted, the legendary, intimidating—okay, terrifying—Draven came to her.

"You're mine for the next month," he'd said.

Startled, she had drawn back from this man who had been with Josh nearly as long as she had, and whose reputation preceded him everywhere in Redstone, and other places where it was useful, as well. Not because she was afraid, as so many were upon one look into those haunted and haunting eyes. She was Redstone, and as such had nothing to fear from this fierce man, but she had no idea what he'd meant.

What he'd meant had been a month of intense, personal training as tough as any boot camp. Tougher, she'd thought when she would fall into bed at night after an exhausting day, suspecting she now understood why, as Eric had told her, they called the most infamous part of Navy SEAL training Hell Week. Because that's what she felt she was getting ready for. Weapons, tactics, physical conditioning, things she'd never even thought about in her relatively sheltered life. She knew she would never have the knack that Draven did, or Sam or any of the others, but she understood; there would be times when she might be the only thing standing between Josh and serious danger. Danger that her skill at the flight controls couldn't get him out of.

They ran countless scenarios in that month, kidnapping,

assassination, snipers, with the entire Redstone Security team pitching in to give her what she needed.

What they gave her in that month, in addition to the tools necessary to protect Josh to some extent, was a much better understanding of the man her husband had been. And she had been unutterably sad that she hadn't had that understanding when he'd been alive. She'd known when she'd fallen—hard—for her SEAL that she was marrying a warrior. She'd understood that he was different than other men, that he was a cut above in skill, dedication and courage. She just hadn't realized quite what it had taken for him to become that man.

But Draven and his team gave her a taste of it in those weeks—driving her, pushing her until one day, too wire-strung to be cautious, she'd actually snuck up behind his observation post and said, "Bang. You're dead."

She'd thought he would be furious. Instead, he had smiled, in those pre-Grace days an occurrence as rare as a rainbow.

"You'll do," he'd said.

Coming from the legendary John Draven, that was tantamount to a medal. And then, quietly, he'd added four words that had destroyed her newly gained composure.

"Eric would be proud."

Her throat had tightened unbearably. At the time she had still been wondering if it would ever end, this ache, this agony. He'd been buried at Arlington for three years, she had told herself, furious at showing what she thought he would think was weakness in front of Draven, of all men. Surely she should be past this by now.

But now, at ten years after, she knew it truly would never end. It had changed, become something she lived with, as much a part of her as her dark hair and eyes. Taken for granted, like the small scar beneath her fringe of bangs, acquired on a rough landing by a fledgling copilot years ago.

And she knew Draven had never thought her weak.

"If the mention of his name didn't move you," he had told her much later, "then it doesn't say much for your love for him."

The unexpected support from this most unexpected source had been worth more than any of the many platitudes she got from others. In fact, she'd realized, the support from her Redstone family had been more helpful and genuine even than from some of her blood family, who had thought her foolish for marrying a man in such a dangerous profession in the first place.

Pinky walked past her, toward the cockpit. She felt the brush of a hand against her backside. It could have been accidental. She doubted it.

"You gonna do something, or just stare in there?" he asked, scowling down at Josh.

"Trying to figure out which wire to cut so the bomb doesn't go off."

Pinky jumped back. "Bomb?" he squeaked. "What bomb?"

Tess smothered a quick smile; as easily as that Josh had let Redstone know—for he knew as well as she did that they were listening by now—that there were no explosives involved.

"Joke," Josh said wryly. "Strung a little tight, aren't you? How long have you worked for Redstone?"

"I—uh—" Pinky stammered.

"Long enough," Brown Shirt snapped.

And again Josh had managed to get across more information, that they were pretending to be Redstone. That had to be puzzling to Draven, she suddenly realized, because he didn't yet know the most crucial thing that they did; that these men hadn't recognized the shaggy, bearded "mechanic" as their quarry.

They didn't even know their trap was sprung.

Chapter 7

"No explosives," Tony Alvera said, as they all listened to the feed, sans St. John who was at the Hawk III controls, freeing Draven to plan. That was a surprise to most; only Draven had known he could fly. But with a simple lift of a dark brow beneath the old-fashioned driver's cap he wore, he'd answered, "I've been with Josh for over twenty years, do you really think he'd let me get by without learning?"

"It's going to be tough getting in there," Draven had said as St. John strapped in. "It's a small airfield."

"I'll get her down." Then, with a grimace, St. John had added, "But with taking off needing about twice as much runway, no promise there."

"I don't care about getting it out," Draven had said, meaning it. "Just get us there."

They'd only been airborne a few minutes before Ryan had the audio running through the onboard system, and turned to the video feeds from the webcams on the Hawk V.

"That's something, at least," Sam said to Alvera's observation about explosives. "They're not bombers."

"But there's something weird going on," Tony said. "Why did Josh ask the guy how long he worked for Redstone? There was nobody else on the plane, was there?"

Logan Beck leaned over and picked up a small, cell-phone-looking device that was actually much more; right now it was a direct link back to Redstone Headquarters. It was a stand-in for the Internet hookup that would have allowed them to use the webcam system to teleconference. But that function was dedicated to the feeds beginning to come in from Josh's plane, under Ryan's quick fingers at the keyboards. Draven considered Barton's precious computers just another tool, only a bit more capricious. Just as semiautomatic pistols could jam, computers could glitch at inopportune moments, and he wanted all the available resources of that system working on only one thing—keeping that precious link open. So they had turned to the handhelds for direct communications with headquarters.

Lilith Alvera, Tony's wife, answered at first ping.

"Have we confirmed the flight schedule, route and manifest?" Beck asked.

The answer came with typical Redstone efficiency. "Yes. Tess took off at the scheduled time, made the drop-off of the two prosthetics for the Veteran's Hospital, met briefly with the head of rehab who took charge of the delivery at the airport. She then proceeded directly to the final destination. Touch down was at eleven-ten."

"The rehab guy didn't decide to tag along by any chance?" Sam asked over Logan's shoulder.

Someone else answered, and despite the situation, Logan smiled at the sound of his wife's voice. "No," Liana said. "I spoke to him personally just after you lifted off. He was headed right back to the hospital for a big media thing scheduled about the donation of the prosthetics."

"We have no permanent staff at that airport, right?" Sam asked.

"Not that we are aware of, but we're still verifying."

Draven frowned; given the thousands of Redstone employees scattered around the globe, that could take a few minutes. Then he realized they had access to a much quicker resource, and walked to the open door of the cockpit.

St. John, a fiercer expression on his face than Draven had seen since the man had come back from his hometown after having defeated his evil father, glanced over his shoulder as if he'd sensed Draven's presence before he spoke.

"Any Redstone personnel at this airport?"

"No."

No equivocating, no pause to think, to remember. Yet Draven didn't doubt the answer for a moment; Josh's mysterious—well, not anymore, since what had happened was well-known now—right-hand man had a knowledge of Redstone that sometimes surpassed even Josh himself.

Draven simply nodded and came back. The others had heard, accepted with the same confidence and moved on.

"Last contact?" Logan was asking.

Lilith again. "Shortly after landing. Tess reported a safe arrival, and said she was settling in to wait for Josh. He'd given her a two-hour window since they were hiking out and ETA could vary."

Draven noticed a muscle along Tony's jaw tighten, and knew he'd heard the undertone beneath Lilith's brisk, businesslike report. While others, including himself, had worked for Redstone longer, Lilith Mercer Alvera had known Josh longer than any of them, known him since she'd been a young teaching assistant barely older than the brilliant, restless teenager she'd tried to guide. She'd sensed his potential from the first day she'd met him. She'd done her best to help him find the path that would fulfill that potential.

And years later, when she'd needed help herself, Josh had

been there for her, bringing the full power of the by then huge entity of Redstone to bear on her behalf.

"Lilith, get me the personnel info on the local sheriff's office, will you? I'm sure we'll be dealing with them before this is over."

"Looking for connections?"

"Exactly."

I do like that woman, Draven thought. He wondered how the world outside Redstone survived with having to explain every little thing to everyone.

"Got it!"

Ryan's exclamation came as the feed from the last of the three webcams came up on the wide-screen monitor. Now they could watch them all simultaneously. Ryan had arranged them from cockpit to galley and work area to main cabin so they were seeing a sideways slice of the plane's interior. Josh had drawn the line at cameras in the stateroom, and given how often Redstone's own had ended up sealing their own very personal futures in that room, there were some on board this plane right now that were glad of that.

They all went utterly silent, watching, and Draven knew that beneath all the assessing, the planning, all the quick thinking that he was certain was taking place in the agile, well-trained minds of his team, was the fear that this would blow up before they got there, that somehow they would fail simply because they hadn't been able to get there in time. Not because of their own speed, he knew St. John was milking every knot from the powerful Redstone jet, but simply because situations like this were inherently volatile, and could go sour at any moment for any reason.

Draven studied the images. Saw the shorter, almost pudgy man in the oddly colored shirt, saw the semiautomatic pistol—it looked like a Browning GP—jammed into his waistband as he held what looked to be a sandwich in one hand and a bottle of something in the other. Alcohol? Would they be dealing with a gunman with impaired abilities, and worse, judgment?

But his attention, as was everyone else's watching, he was sure, was centered mainly on the woman in the galley, and the tall, lanky man kneeling on the floor of the cockpit, staring into the hole created by the removal of a section of the flooring.

"Hill to Airborne."

Taylor Hill's voice crackled over the handheld. Logan still held it, so he answered. "Airborne here."

That would be their designation until they landed, and would become the Ground Team.

"Getting the feed Barton routed. The wiring schematic of the Hawk V was accessed from the onboard computer."

"When?"

"Within the last twenty minutes. And it was still open when the duress alarm was sent."

"Copy," Beck said, looking at the others to confirm they'd all heard.

"Now, why would they want access to the wiring? No bomb, Josh already established that," Draven muttered, never taking his eyes off the screen.

"I'm thinking of quitting this job."

Tess Machado's sudden words over the speakers had them all flicking glances at each other in silent query. No one registered knowledge, and in a split second they were all refocused on the screen. With the webcam's angle they could only see Tess's right side as she fussed with something in the galley, but her voice had been crystal clear.

They saw Josh, still kneeling beside the opening in the flooring, go very still.

"Flight attendant jobs are overrated," she said then.

This round of glances was accompanied by raised eyebrows. Flight attendant? The best pilot at Redstone, short of Josh himself?

"What the hell is going on?" Tony murmured.

I wish I knew, thought Draven, and leaned in closer.

Josh's mind was racing as he fiddled beneath the floor, as if he were looking for something specific amid the spaghetti-like mass of cables and thinner wires. Tess's words echoed in his ears. He knew what she'd been trying to relay, he just wasn't sure yet what it meant. Or more important, how to turn it to their advantage.

Tess knew as well as he did that by now they were under observation, and that Draven and the rest were watching every move, and listening, as well.

"I've never felt valued, you know?" she said, and Josh realized she was aiming her comments at Pinky. "I'd like a perk now and then, an extra day off, a flight to see my family on one of these fancy jets, maybe even a raise."

"That's how they are, those fat cats," Pinky said, as Josh pondered the fact that Tess had had all of those things, and within the past month. The first two to visit her sister, Francie, who had just made her an aunt, and the last just because she deserved it.

"I'd like to get treated like he treats his pilot."

Josh fiddled with the plastic clip that held several of the smaller wires separate from the bigger cables, but his attention was fastened on Tess's odd conversation. Why was she even talking to these guys, let alone as she was?

"I'll bet he treats that guy with some respect," Brown Shirt said, glancing at her.

"Absolutely," Tess said. "That's the best job in the world. To that pilot, Josh Redstone is the best there is. The best boss... the best man. That pilot would do absolutely anything for him."

Josh froze. He barely managed not to look at her. He wasn't sure what she was trying to do, but there was no doubting the absolute sincerity of her words. He knew Tess, cool-headed, unflappable Tess, and there had to be a point to all this gushing.

Was it gushing if she meant it?

Josh shook off the thought. Tess was his rock, the person he could always turn to, the person he depended on for his personal grounding the way he depended on St. John to keep Redstone grounded. He couldn't afford to lose that in some tangle of emotion she wouldn't want.

"Thanks for the warning," Brown Shirt said, sounding thoughtful. "When's he supposed to get here, the pilot?"

There was the briefest pause during which Josh guessed Tess was thinking fast.

"Oh," she said, almost airily, "he doesn't have to show up until the big man does."

"They stick together, those kind," Pinky said with a sneer Josh was all too familiar with, the expression of the perpetually offended.

And belatedly he realized that both Pinky and Brown Shirt were focused on Tess. And that that had been her plan all along, to distract them. Swiftly he reached under the floor board, swiped his right thumb over the miniature scanner, heard the faint click of the lock releasing. He grabbed the pistol, secured in the box with a quick release clip, and with a glance to be sure the two men were still looking at Tess, he pulled it free. Quickly, he slipped it into an inside pocket of his jacket, a deep pocket normally reserved for flight logs.

He dived back into the wiring, his actions apparently unnoticed as the men focused on Tess.

That he could understand; he couldn't imagine a man breathing who wouldn't rather look at Tess. The brightest moments of the sometimes long, work-laden flights were when she would try to cheer him up with some unexpected quip or a complete non sequitur of trivia injected into a serious conversation, just to see his startled blink.

Tess was, in fact, the only person who could consistently

make him laugh. Others made him smile, some could bemuse or amuse him, but it was Tess, with her quick wit and wry humor who made him throw back his head and laugh out loud. They were moments he treasured not just because of their rarity, but because he treasured her.

In the beginning, he'd simply appreciated her skill with anything that flew, and admired her quick, adaptive mind. And he'd liked that she and Elizabeth had bonded so quickly. Later he realized he himself had come to depend on her, on her way of giving things a slight tweak, making him look at them a little differently, usually giving him clarity if not the actual answer he'd been seeking.

An odd flash of memory shot through his mind, vivid and sharp. A night just a week ago, in his office at Redstone Headquarters, when Tess had done just that, said one simple thing that had turned the entire problem he'd been pondering just enough that he saw a different facet of it, a facet he knew instantly was the way to the solution. He'd been on the phone to St. John and point man Noah Rider in seconds, the path to resolving the materials issue clearly lit now.

When he'd finished, Tess had been gone. She instinctively seemed to know when he needed the space, just as Elizabeth always had.

He'd leaned back in his chair, his gaze straying to the portrait that hung on the opposite wall. The image of the lovely woman with the warm brown eyes was as familiar as the back of his hand. No collection of oil colors could truly capture the lively vivacity that went along with the down-to-earth wit and gentle, kind heart, but the artist had done a decent job. The glint of humor was in her eyes, and the beginnings of that wide smile on her face.

"You'd be proud of her, El," he'd murmured to the image that was all he had left of the woman he'd once loved so deeply. "She's become everything you always said she would. A force to be reckoned with, our Tess."

He knew it was true. Elizabeth had had a blood sister, but they'd never been close, and there couldn't have been two more different women; where Elizabeth had been kind, generous and good-natured, Phyllis was cold, calculating and, he had to admit, greedy. And had unfortunately raised her son in the same mold.

But Tess had been, in Elizabeth's words, the sister of her heart, the one she would have chosen if it were possible. When she knew the end was close, she'd instructed Josh to always look out for Tess. He would have anyway, for her own sake, but he'd promised nevertheless.

"And she'll look out for you," Elizabeth had said, her voice already weak. "In due time, you'll realize. I trust you both to find your way."

The oddity of those words hadn't struck him until much later, when it was over and the woman who had been the sun in his life was long gone.

He shook his head sharply; this was hardly the time to get lost in memories. If he knew Draven, and he did, they were already mobilized and on their way. And when things started to happen, they would happen fast, and they'd better be ready.

Brown Shirt had turned his attention back to Josh, and was watching his every move. If not for Tess's quick thinking and diversion, he never would have gotten to that weapon. And he nearly smiled inwardly; she'd once again shown her cleverness in playing into the apparent perceptions of these men. If they thought they were dealing with some not-too-bright, helpless female, they were in for a big surprise.

Because outside Redstone Security, there was no one he'd rather have at his side in a fight than Tess.

Chapter 8

It had seemed like a good plan. Playing into the very mistaken preconceptions these men seemed to have about Josh could only help, Tess thought, and would cement the fiction that he was yet to arrive. But even knowing what was at stake, she found it hard to talk about him so negatively.

"The opposite," she had said, "that's what I'd like."

And had proceeded to complain about her supposedly absent boss by describing the polar opposite of the man he really was.

It was only when she was well into it that she realized what she was betraying; by describing Josh in terms that were obviously the reverse of the truth, and of her view of him, she was showing just how deeply her feelings for him went. Not that their two captors would realize that, but she was very much afraid Josh would.

"He's rude, and abrupt and impatient with people," she said, grimacing inwardly as she described the man who was unfailingly polite, patient and infinitely generous with his

valuable time. And when Josh glanced at her, one brow raised
slightly, she gave a dramatic sigh so unlike herself that she
knew he couldn't miss it.

Brown Shirt wasn't buying it completely, she could sense
that. On some level he no doubt suspected she was angling for
their sympathy, or trying to save herself by aligning herself
with them against Josh. Pinky, on the other hand, seemed
perfectly willing to go along, as if everyone in the world must
hate their boss, simply because that's the way he thought.

"What I'd like is a good boss," she said, thinking she'd
just keep chattering to cover Josh's actions—she thought he'd
gotten the pistol, in fact was sure of it because he was standing
now—as long as they'd let her, no matter that chatter was
totally foreign to her nature. "You know, one that cares about
his employees, takes care of them, pays well and gives them
respect."

In other words, Josh, she thought. She flicked a quick look
at him; surely he had to know what she was doing, describing
exactly who he really was.

"No such animal," Pinky said with a snort as Josh again
glanced their way before explaining briefly to Brown Shirt
that he needed to check something in the main cabin.

Josh was headed toward her. She didn't expect a move,
there was no way he could do anything with the two men right
there, watching. The weapon he'd retrieved was hers, the 9mm
Kahr P9 she'd picked to fit her smaller hands, and because
she liked the balance and the grips. But she knew ruefully
well that Josh wouldn't hand off the only weapon they had so
far to her. He'd lived off and on in some rural areas, hunting,
and she knew Draven had refined his skills, so Josh was far
from helpless.

"At the rate we're going," she grumbled, "we could have
waited to leave from down south at noon and still have made
it before he will."

Josh gave her a quick sideways glance as Pinky made

another nasty comment about arrogant CEOs, and she knew he'd picked up her inference that if the security team had mobilized immediately—and she knew they had—they would be arriving very soon.

"Keep an eye on her," Brown Shirt said to Pinky. Then, apparently realizing that didn't fit with the facade they were presenting to the "mechanic," added hastily, "We wouldn't want her getting hurt, now would we?"

"No," Josh said as Brown Shirt followed him past the galley into the cabin, "we wouldn't."

Something in his voice sent a shiver up her spine. She'd heard that tone before. When he'd learned Harlan was missing in Nicaragua. When a mole selling Redstone secrets had threatened Ian Gamble. When Lilith had been in danger. It was steely, implacable determination. And no one, just no one, stopped a determined Josh Redstone. Tess knew that better than anyone.

The fact that they were presenting this facade to the man they knew only as a worker had to mean something, she thought. If they were totally ruthless, wouldn't they simply have taken "Michael" hostage, too? Did that mean they weren't pros? They certainly didn't act like it.

Maybe they were just a couple of disgruntled failures grabbing what they saw as an opportunity. Had they heard Josh Redstone was here and come hunting? Or was it even simpler, had they just seen the Hawk V and figured whoever was flying on the private jet had to be worth something? Or was it some combination of both?

She supposed it still didn't matter, the how of it. It was the fact of it she and Josh had to deal with.

And you can chalk anything you say up to the necessity of the moment, she told herself.

She put a little whine into her voice and said, trying to keep at least Pinky's attention off Josh as he stopped in front of the polished wood panel that masked the power panel for the auxiliary systems, "There must be a boss somewhere who cares about his people."

"You think somebody like this guy—" Pinky took a step out of the galley and gestured at the interior of the plane "—cares about anybody but himself?"

"That," Tess said, slowly and with an almost fierce emphasis, more than loud enough for Josh to hear, "would make him a very, very special man. The kind you'd walk through fire for."

Josh paused as he fiddled with more wiring. Turning to look at her, his voice almost deadly quiet, he spoke to her for the first time since she'd begun her charade.

"If he was that kind of man, he wouldn't let you."

She wasn't sure if it was a declaration, or a warning. What she was sure was that he meant it. And she knew Draven had, if anything, understated when he'd told her all those years ago that the toughest part of her job in a situation like this would be to get Josh to let her put herself in danger for him.

"He's going to get himself hurt trying to keep her from getting hurt," Beck muttered.

"She doesn't need his help," Alvera said. "She did great in our training, she can handle anything just about as well as any of us could."

"But Josh doesn't know that, does he?" Reeve put in. "He knows we absconded with her for a while, taught her to shoot, but not the details of what we put her through."

They all looked at Draven, who shrugged. "Josh wouldn't have okayed it. You know how he feels about bodyguards."

"Same way my husband did," Sam said. "But I'm glad you did what you did. Tess is as good as a secret weapon now."

"And she would lay down her life for him," Reeve said. The two women exchanged glances Draven noted, but didn't quite understand.

"We all would," Alvera said with unwavering conviction.

"And you'd all do Josh a lot of good dead, wouldn't you?" Draven pointed out.

"And so," Sam said, turning a steady look on her boss, "would you."

Draven resisted for a moment, but he knew every one of his team here knew the truth. They wouldn't be on the team if they didn't.

"My job is to protect Redstone, and I'd walk through fire to do it." His voice harshened despite himself. "But I'd stand in that fire and burn for Josh."

"ETA twenty minutes," St. John's voice said over the intercom.

"Facts," Draven said abruptly.

"Two men, two weapons, Josh and Tess aboard," Sam said quickly.

"Assumptions," he said in the same tone. "Beyond that they don't even recognize Josh."

"They don't know Tess is the pilot," Reeve said. Draven nodded; Tess's words had made that clear enough it almost went into the fact category.

"Josh is now armed," Alvera said; although they hadn't actually seen the weapon, they'd observed Josh's movements in the cockpit and there was no other logical explanation. "And," he added with a gesture at the screen Ryan Barton was still monitoring with a fierce concentration, "in a minute or two he'll have the second weapon, which he'll hopefully pass to Tess."

"The cockpit weapon is hers," Draven said, his eyes on the screen. "Her weapon of choice."

That had been on his instruction, since Tess was most likely to be in the cockpit. It was a minute point, but having a weapon you were familiar with and that had been sighted in and maintained by you could make the hairsbreadth of difference between life and death in a situation like this.

But the explanation didn't negate the fact that getting Josh to let any of his people take personal risks for his sake was an iffy prospect at best. And this wasn't just any of his people, this was Tess.

"She'll get it from him," Sam predicted.

Draven nodded. He knew her well. And they'd trained her well. And he knew the fact that Tess was also a hostage only compounded his team's ferocity.

"Speculation," he snapped out.

"They're idiots," Beck said, earning him a quick grin from most of the team.

"It does seem," Reeve said in a more assessing tone, "that they are either stupid, careless or at the least amateurs."

"Trying to take hostage a man you don't even recognize when he's standing in front of you?" Beck retorted. "Yeah, I'd say so."

They spent the next ten minutes of the flight going over the various possibilities that had been presented by Josh and Tess's clever maneuvers from on board the Hawk V. From the armed men's responses to their various comments, they'd gathered the basics, although Draven warned it was, at this point, all speculation based on the assumption they were correctly interpreting what they'd heard and seen.

The last five minutes before they touched down they spent silently arming themselves, each of them with their own personal choices, from Sam's Sig to Beck's Glock 21. Additional weapons followed; they would assess carefully first, but if the time came when they had to move fast, none of them wanted to have to stop to gear up.

They began to drop. Draven knew the Hawk III was large for this small airfield, but it was especially equipped and stocked to handle almost anything short of an all out war. He wished they had Tess to get them on the ground; she could put the big jet down safely on runways any sane pilot would tell you were far too short for it. But no one at Redstone underestimated St. John, either.

"Brace," that man said on the intercom, warning them all this was going to be an abrupt procedure.

And he set the plane down, not with Tess's featherlight finesse but with a solid thump that spoke of his mood, and laid on the brakes almost instantly. Wedged in the cockpit doorway, Draven caught a glimpse of Josh's plane sitting off the main taxiway at the north end of the strip.

As soon as the jet was slowed enough he would tell St. John—an oddity in itself—to stay here at the opposite end of the small airfield; if the men aboard the Hawk V hadn't seen them land, no sense calling attention to the fact. The unmarked jet—plain-wrapped, Beck called it—stood out enough for its size alone at this small airport.

But before he could open his mouth St. John was doing just that, and Draven chided himself ruefully for not realizing the man had already thought of everything.

"I don't think they saw us, or they don't care," Ryan said, his gaze still glued to the wide-screen, multipicture monitor he'd braced through the hard landing. "They didn't react at all. Tess is still talking, and they're paying more attention to her than to Josh, even."

"They don't think the 'mechanic' is a threat," Sam said.

"Looks like they wish Tess would shut up," Ryan said.

"I'm sure Tess would like to," Reeve said. "Babbling is so not her."

"But it's working," Ryan said, never taking his eyes off the screen. "She— Wait!"

They all turned as the young computer genius yelped.

"Josh saw us!" he yelped. Sam leaned over his shoulder. "He just turned and looked right at the camera and did something with his hand."

Draven spun around and took two long strides to the monitor. "What did he do, exactly?"

Ryan lifted his right hand and slashed it across his neck from left to right.

"Doesn't that mean to stop engines?" Ryan asked. "Like the ground-crew signal?"

"It's context determined," Draven said. "It's a hand signal borrowed from ground forces. Jim taught them to Josh years ago." He remembered Jim telling him about it, that it had been a way to share with his little brother the excitement he felt at going into special ops.

"So here it means...?" Ryan asked.

Draven answered quietly, saying what they all already knew.

"Danger zone."

Chapter 9

Tess knew Josh had taken advantage of their two captors'
momentary attention to the sparkling water she had spilled.
She knew he had retrieved a second weapon from its compartment beside the wiring panel. She knew they hadn't
noticed a thing.

What she didn't know was if Josh would manage to overcome his instinctual, fiercely protective nature and do what she
knew Draven would demand, give her the cockpit weapon.

As she cleaned up, she pondered ways to make the transfer.
Finally, she settled on one that seemed feasible; it would get
the job done and further cement their image of her as a rather
brainless and clumsy ditz.

She looked around the galley as if searching for something.
After a moment, with a shrug—and even though there were
several towels in the drawer next to the small refrigerator—she
tugged her shirttail out and dried her hands on it. She left it
out; it hung below the hip on her petite frame.

She started out of the galley toward the main cabin, only to have Pinky frown and step in front of her.

"I have to replace that water out of the storage locker, or Mr. Redstone will be furious."

Pinky laughed, using a foul word to describe the man he had no idea was mere feet away.

"Please," Tess said, trying to inject as much fear into her voice as she could, a difficult task given what she was feeling was anger and disgust. "I don't want him mad at me."

That a spilled bottle of water would be the least of any sane man's worries when confronted with two armed men intent on taking him hostage didn't seem to occur to the man. And Tess's opinion of his intelligence—or lack thereof—solidified as she crossed the cabin to the cabinet at the far corner of the main cabin, near where Josh was pretending to work.

She got out the bottle to complete the deception, and with a surreptitious move slipped a wine opener into her pocket; it might be small, but the blade used to cut the wrapping on the bottles could be useful. Then she turned as if to go back to the galley, looking down at the bottle in her hands. And walked right into Josh.

"Oh! I'm sorry, I—"

"Easy, there," Josh said, steadying her with his right hand. For an instant they just stood there, pressed together from knee to chest—well, Josh's chest, since she was so much shorter—and Tess's heart began to hammer in a way that had embarrassingly little to do with the situation they were in. Which was beyond foolish, and she tried to quash her response fiercely, all the while hoping Josh would assume, if he noticed, that it was the situation that had her adrenaline pumping wildly.

And then, after what seemed like a long, drawn out moment she was certain had really only been a couple of seconds, Josh's left hand, the one away from their captors, moved to her other shoulder. Slowly, almost as if he were reluctant to separate from her.

But in the process, he slipped the cockpit pistol to her. As he released her, she palmed the small weapon in her right hand, then slid it carefully into her waistband. The now untucked Redstone shirt was loose enough and long enough to hide it easily. The fact that it also masked her curved shape was a bonus, given Pinky's frequent, too-intent stares.

She glanced up at Josh, relieved that he'd followed Draven's strict rules. That he'd done it reluctantly was clear in his expression as he looked down at her. She supposed following his own simple rule, of getting out of his people's way and letting them do their jobs, was sometimes harder than people realized.

"Careful," he murmured.

She didn't miss that he meant much more than her feigned stumble.

"You about done here?" Brown Shirt asked Josh. Impatience crackled in his voice and was clearly evident on his face. Great, Tess thought. The stupid one's nasty, and the smarter one is edgy. Not an encouraging combination.

"Still have to isolate the problem in all that wiring," Josh said easily. "No skin off my nose if the guy's got to wait around. He's kept you guys waiting all afternoon, hasn't he?"

"Serves him right," Pinky agreed, almost gleeful.

Brown Shirt ignored his partner. And when he looked at Josh, it was still with a trace of suspicion. Tess hoped it was because "Michael" was taking too long, and not that he was on the verge of recognizing him as their true quarry.

She felt much better now that she had the little eight-round Kahr within reach. Cooler, calmer. Josh would never want or allow anyone to die for him if he could stop it, but Tess knew practically anyone in Redstone would, if necessary.

She would, if necessary.

When the words coalesced in her mind, it wasn't a revelation. Her feelings for Josh were simply a fact of life. The life she would never have had if not for this man. And if she'd spent a bit too much of it lately longing for the impossible, then that was her fault, not his. Her fault that she'd committed the sin of being impossibly cliché, falling in love with her rich, unattainable boss.

Her only consolation was that he never had to know.

Her only regret was, that if things went wrong, he never would.

The manager of the small airfield gaped at the Redstone team as they stood out of sight of the rest of the field, behind a hangar barely large enough to conceal the Hawk III. One look at John Draven's eyes had the man nodding his head as he was questioned.

"Seen anyone you don't know around this afternoon?"

"People come and go," the man said, clearly puzzled. "It's an airport."

It was two short runways with an air sock and a Quonset hut, but Draven wisely didn't point that out.

"Anyone not connected to a plane?"

"I wouldn't know. I've been doing paperwork in the office all afternoon."

"So anyone could walk out on to the apron where the planes are parked?"

"Well…" The man's voice trailed off, and he shifted his feet as if uncomfortable. "It's not like terrorists are going to show up *here*," he finally said.

"Anyone else here who might have seen anything?"

"We're a small operation," the man said defensively. "Full-time, there's only me and Jay, guy who runs the fuel truck, and washes planes for extra cash. But he ran into town for supplies, since we weren't expecting anyone to need him."

The man was beginning to look a little bit suspicious,

and Draven decided there was no real help here. He told the man that they were here to meet with Mr. Redstone when he returned to his plane, and that they wished to keep that quiet. The Redstone name had its usual effect, the man's expression cleared.

"Oh," he said.

Draven's glance flicked to Samantha Gamble; he'd noticed the man's gaze straying repeatedly to the leggy blonde. She never hesitated, just stepped over to the man and smiled that megawatt smile.

"It's sort of a test exercise, you know?" she said genially. "Like you probably have to do here, you have to make sure everything runs smoothly when things are fine, to be sure they will when they're not."

"Oh. Yeah. Sure."

The man was gaping openly at Sam, who pretended he was utterly charming.

Whether it was the Redstone name or Sam, Draven didn't know. What mattered was that it worked; moments later they were alone to assess which of the possible plans they'd put together on the flight might work.

St. John came down the steps of the Hawk III and joined them. The scar along the right side of his jaw jumped, betraying his inner tension in a way Draven had never seen before.

But then, he guessed most of them were tense in a way they had never been before.

"Radio," St. John said. "Mac's a half hour out."

Draven nodded, unsurprised; he'd known McClaren wouldn't waste any time, and he was probably flying his own Hawk V, the second one ever built.

"Rider's with him," St. John added.

Again Draven nodded, the presence of Redstone's premier point man no surprise, either. He'd known that once word got out he was going to have trouble keeping all of Redstone from showing up. Down to the lowest person in the hierarchy the sense of family held, and that family was unfailingly loyal to the man who made it all possible.

"Recon," Draven said. The team went still, waiting. "Low profile, until we get the lay of things." He considered for an instant. The women—less of a threat and more likely to be overlooked?

As if any man would overlook those two, he thought, looking at the two blondes, one tall, leggy, athletic and one tinier, almost fragile-looking, but both beautiful.

"A couple," he murmured, processing quickly. "Hikers, I think. Covers backpacks."

He needed to be here to assess and work out the plan. Not Alvera, too dangerous looking. And Beck had never quite lost the cop demeanor. The best choice would probably be boy-next-door Barton, but he had no security training, and they needed him on the tech gear. Right now he was downloading the aerial shot of the area that Draven had requested.

If Rand were here, he'd be perfect, but he was still on his way. That left him only one choice. And while he was not a trained agent any more than Barton was, he'd grown up harder, tougher and had the best logistical mind Draven had ever encountered.

"Reeve," he said, and the petite agent nodded. She grabbed up the pack sitting at her feet. In it, Draven knew, were weapons of various sorts, and other tactical gear that might be useful.

Then he looked at St. John and raised a brow. If St. John was surprised it didn't show, and he merely nodded. Jessa may have changed his life, even gotten him to occasionally shed his considerable armor, but he was more than capable of putting it back on when necessary.

No one questioned Draven's decision. They were too well trained, and had, he knew, utter and complete faith in him.

On this mission more than any other, he would see that it was deserved.

"Between them," Sam said with a crooked smile as she looked from her boss to St. John, "they talk enough for any eighth of a person."

Echoing smiles flashed as St. John shrugged on the pack Draven handed him with a quick description of the contents. The quip would have seemed awkward if they were anything less than Redstone. Draven knew they all were certain they would get this done, and bring Josh and Tess home safely. The joking was just their way of confirming that. He knew his team well.

Reeve held out her hand, continuing the joking. "Come along, my love, and we shall stroll the tarmac like Rick and Ilsa."

"And have Zach on my ass? No thanks," St. John quipped back, startling them all. But he took Reeve's hand and they headed toward the Hawk V, indeed strolling as if they had nothing more on their minds than togetherness as they set out on a ramble through the wilderness.

It had begun.

Chapter 10

"What's taking so long?"

"Why in such a hurry?" Josh asked Brown Shirt mildly.

He'd settled down to work behind the panel in the main cabin; the mass of wiring that fed out from it looked incredibly complex, and he figured it would justify several minutes of fiddling. He'd already isolated the cable he wanted, but couldn't do what else he needed with the man hovering, watching every move.

"Just finish, will you?" Brown Shirt snapped.

Josh lifted one shoulder in a half shrug. "No reason to rush when he's not even back yet." He glanced at Tess, held her gaze as he added, "It's not like there's a whole entourage here waiting to make a move."

He saw the briefest flicker in her dark eyes as she registered his meaning, and he knew she knew the troops had arrived. He guessed she had suspected; she'd heard the plane, and he was willing to bet she'd recognized it as the Hawk III just from the sound, so finely tuned were her ears to the differences in various engines.

"He'll want to leave, get back to his fancy office, as soon as he gets here," Brown Shirt said.

"Hmm," Josh said, knowing his office was far from fancy.

"The angel flight," Tess said softly.

Josh hadn't forgotten. The latest possible wheels-up time that would allow them to make it in time was rapidly approaching.

"Angel flight? What the hell is that?"

Tess looked at Brown Shirt. Josh could almost feel her quick mind racing. If she explained, it might throw a wrench in their perceptions of their target, and he guessed she couldn't decide if that would be good or bad. Knowing Tess, she wanted to hurl the facts at them, that a child might die because of their actions, but her innate common sense was telling her that if they were the kind of men who would care about that, they wouldn't be doing this in the first place.

Josh took the decision out of her hands. "P.R. stunt," he said, using the accusation his detractors—the people who couldn't seem to resist attacking success—sometimes used.

Brown Shirt considered, then nodded. "Figures."

But a scheduled angel flight was sacrosanct. Everyone at Redstone knew that, but Josh figured under current cirumstances a nudge wouldn't hurt. He shifted slightly so he was directly facing the webcam. "But there are a lot of Redstone planes and several pilots. Somebody will step in."

It was as good as an order, and Josh knew his people on the other end would know it. In fact, if St. John hadn't already handled it, he would be surprised.

He turned back to the wiring, wondering just how long he could stretch this out.

"Hey," Pinky said suddenly, "there's some people walking around outside."

Brown Shirt wheeled around and strode across the cabin to peer out the window where his collaborator was standing beside Tess. Josh quickly grabbed up the wire cutters from the small selection of tools Brown Shirt had allowed him to retrieve from the locker down the corridor.

"Just some sappy couple," Brown Shirt snorted. "Holding hands, come to moon over the rich man's toy."

"He's probably telling her he'll buy her one someday," Pinky said with a laugh. "That's what women want to hear."

Josh saw Tess take the chance to look, as well.

"She's a tiny little thing," Tess said. "And you don't see caps like he's wearing very often anymore."

"Just shut up, and stay in the kitchen where you belong," Brown Shirt said to her, sharply.

St. John? Josh thought, masking his surprise as he tugged at the target cable. Reeve, obviously, she was still part of the security team, but what was St. John doing here? Didn't he realize he needed to stay out of this, stay safe? He was the only one who could step in at Redstone if this turned ugly and something happened to him.

Tess glanced at him then, and he gave her a barely perceptible nod to indicate he'd understood. What he wanted to do was salute her; she'd gotten her message across without saying a single thing that roused suspicion. In the role she'd set for herself, a chatty, not too bright, low woman on the totem pole, she'd put herself so far out of the threat category that neither man was worrying about her anymore.

Not that Pinky had forgotten her, Josh thought with an inward grimace. He knew exactly what that guy was thinking every time he looked at her. And he didn't much like it.

The two men were still looking out the window, and he took advantage of their focus to quickly cut the cable he was after, then shred the protective coating as best he could, to make it look as if it had worn naturally.

"Should I go chase them off?" Pinky asked.

"And be seen? No," Brown Shirt snapped.

Pinky shrugged. "Just figured that'd be what the big shot would do. Never let the peons get too close."

Josh set the cutters down and had both hands back amid the wiring before Brown Shirt came back to resume his supervision.

"You find the problem yet?" the man asked.

"I think so," Josh said, tugging at the cable he'd just stuffed back down behind the wall. The newly cut end, looking suitably ragged, pulled free.

Brown Shirt frowned. "What's that?"

"Let's just say this plane isn't going anywhere anytime soon, no matter what Redstone wants."

Pinky laughed, almost gleefully. Obviously, the idea of the plane not being able to take off didn't bother him. Josh filed that away in his mind as he let the cable—which, in fact, only controlled the floor lighting—dangle in plain view, not sure what the knowledge meant or how to use it. Yet. He was sure Draven was doing the same on the outside.

"How did that happen?" Brown Shirt asked.

"Cheap materials," Josh said with a shrug, guessing this man knew nothing about the standards of Redstone. "The whole cable will have to be replaced. That's going to take a while."

"Forget it," Brown Shirt said impatiently.

Josh schooled his expression to one of mild curiosity. "This plane can't fly."

"I said forget it."

"It got here, didn't it?" Pinky said. Maybe the man wasn't quite as stupid as he seemed, Josh thought. Or he just had that kind of instinctive shrewdness that some animals had. Like rats, he added silently.

"Our landing here was very rough," Tess said. "That pilot really bounced us around. Could that have done it?"

Josh looked at the woman who regularly set down bigger

and heavier planes than this so softly passengers sometimes weren't sure they were down until they began to slow.

"Could have," he said with a nod. "You can't throw machinery like this around."

In fact, the Hawks were tough, durable and had enough redundancy built in to keep them airworthy beyond the capacity of most planes, private or commercial. But he wasn't thinking of that. He was thinking of what Brown Shirt had just confirmed with his reaction.

Their intent had never been to get airborne.

"This is ridiculous," Brown Shirt announced.

Tess went very still. Josh was sitting at the desk, on the pretext of writing up an estimate for the repair Brown Shirt didn't seem concerned about. It hadn't taken her long to arrive at the same conclusion she was certain Josh already had; these men had never intended for the plane to take off. She only hoped Draven had been able to see clearly enough to realize the same thing.

"I'm sick of waiting for this jerk. Who the hell does he think he is, anyway?"

He's the man who designed and built this plane, and an empire that helps keep the world working, a man who never took the easy way out, and he's worth a million of you, Tess thought.

She glanced at Josh, who had also paused in his work. "With my luck," he said, with an air of disgust, "after I've done all this work, he'll bring in somebody else to do the repair."

"That would figure," Brown Shirt said, distracted just enough after his burst of anger.

Tess seized the chance to further diffuse the sudden volatility. "I'm tired of waiting, too," she said quickly. "I need the head, even if I'm not supposed to use it."

"You can't even use his big, executive bathroom?" Pinky exclaimed. "What a prick!"

She started walking toward the back of the plane, where the head and stateroom were.

"Go with her," Brown Shirt said to Pinky.

"My pleasure," Pinky said, his eyes lighting up with a glow Tess had caught before, one that made her decidedly edgy. Brown Shirt worried her, but this man simply made her skin crawl. He kept brushing up against her, touching her, and she wanted to break every one of his fingers.

"Some privacy, please," she said when he held back the door she tried to close.

"Aw, now, honey, don't be a prude," Pinky said with a leer.

"Do you really want to watch me change tampons?" she asked sweetly, nearly laughing as the man recoiled. She pulled the door shut, snapped the lock and leaned against the inside of it, letting out a deep breath.

No time to relax, she ordered herself and quickly walked across the small but efficient room. She thought it might be wise to actually make use of the facility, and did so as she loosened the panel next to the head where Draven had ordered it placed for just that reason.

"Clever, clever man, our Draven," Tess murmured as she quickly had the third pistol in her hands.

She washed her hands, leaving the water running longer than necessary as she thought. They had three weapons between them now. Part of her training with the security team had been to shoot left-handed nearly as well as right. She'd understood the theory at the time, but never in her life had she ever expected she might have to actually rely on that training. And she certainly had never wanted to.

Not, she thought with a wry twist of her mouth, that the thought of shutting Pinky up—and keeping his nasty hands off her—didn't hold a very definite appeal.

Josh would know she'd gone for the weapon in here. The question was, what did they do now? Every scenario they'd run during that training had had keeping Josh safe as the goal, but every scenario had been different in one basic way from the situation they were in now.

No one, not even Draven, had ever imagined a scenario where the threat didn't even recognize the target.

Chapter 11

Sometime in the past five minutes, Brown Shirt had changed. He was still spouting off as he had been, but there was a new, angry determination in his voice.

"This is ridiculous," the man exclaimed.

The entire group that was gathered back in the cabin of the big Hawk III went still, including Draven. Until now Brown Shirt had been the calm one; if he was losing it...

Their number had grown now. Harlan McClaren's Hawk V, a twin to Josh's except for not having the trademark Redstone fleet paint job, had set down about five minutes ago, later than the ETA he'd originally given St. John on the radio.

But that was explained when the passengers had deplaned; the famous treasure hunter and Redstone point man Noah Rider they'd expected, after St. John's report. Gabe Taggert and Ian Gamble were a surprise, although Draven knew the one time navy captain could be a valuable asset. And Ian... well, you never knew with Ian. His kind of quirky mind could be invaluable. Rand Singleton, the tall blond head of

Redstone Security Northwest, and who could be Samantha
Gamble's masculine twin, had been a bigger surprise, but a
very welcome one.

"I made a stop and picked up Gabe and Ian at the home
field, then got a call from Rand and picked him up in Merced,"
Mac explained.

Sam had taken the unexpected arrival of her husband well.
She'd merely lifted a brow, prompting Ian to say, "He's with
Ryan's mom." Sam had nodded and left it at that.

Draven marveled at her cool. Baby Josh was her first and
only child, and her question wasn't how could you leave him,
but simply where was he. She trusted Ian to have made the best
decision possible. There had been a time not so long ago when
Draven would have found that kind of trust unbelievable.

Not anymore, he thought, allowing himself a glance at the
final and most unexpected passenger who had gotten off Mac's
plane. His own wife, who had managed the steep plane steps
with the grace she'd been named for despite the prosthetic
foot that was one of Ian's most famous accomplishments.

His heart had nearly stopped in his throat at the sight of her.
The goal was always to avoid any violence or weapons, but
that was a goal it wasn't always possible to meet in situations
like this. Before he could open his mouth she'd looked up
at him, brushed tousled dark bangs away from those huge
blue eyes and forestalled his objections. "I know airports.
Otherwise, I'm out of the way."

He couldn't argue with that. Because his brilliant wife did
indeed know airports; she built them. And the knowledge
might come in handy.

Trust, he thought again. He trusted everyone here, either
to do their job, or let the others do theirs, even if it might include risk. He trusted them as he hadn't trusted a team since
he'd been in uniform, all those years ago.

A sudden image flashed through his mind of his best friend,
body shattered by a land mine, looking up at him with eyes

that were already losing the vivid light of life, and extracting that promise.

"I'll look out for him, Jimmy. I'll look out for your little brother."

And he had. For twenty years now, the safety of James Redstone's little brother had been his most important mission. That it had expanded into something that far exceeded even his wildest dreams didn't change that basic task.

"If they're losing it, we have to move," Alvera said now, staring at the scenes steadily unrolling on the video monitor.

"And do what?" Reeve asked.

"No ransom demand because as far as they know, they don't have him yet," Sam said.

"If it comes to that, pay it," Mac said. "I'll pay it myself in an instant for Josh."

"Except that he'd take your head off," Noah Rider put in.

"I'll deal with that after he's safe," Mac said.

"We're not going there yet," Draven said after listening to the exchanges.

"Why doesn't he just leave?" Beck asked. "They think he's just a mechanic, why doesn't he just make an excuse and get the hell out?"

"And leave Tess there with them? Not Josh."

"And especially not Tess," Sam said with an emphasis that put words to what Draven guessed they were all thinking; Tess and Josh had been a wish they had all made at one time or another.

"When this is over, those two better get their act together," Grace said sternly.

At her words Beck glanced at the others, read their expressions. He looked rueful as he said, "Oh. Sorry. New-guy syndrome."

"Not your fault," Reeve said with a wry twist of her mouth.

"They do their damnedest to ignore what's obvious to the rest of us."

"True, but not our mission now," Draven said, drawing them back, knowing that no one could will their personal worry about Josh out of their minds, but also knowing it was essential to act with cool heads and not out of emotions.

Reeve and St. John had reported back after their circuit of Josh's plane and the area surrounding it, saying that there was no outward sign it had been tampered with, and more important, no sign at all that there was anyone on the ground connected to the two men aboard. They appeared to be working alone.

In fact, they'd said, there was no one on the ground at all; the airport manager hadn't lied when he'd said there was only him and the fueler.

But there were now a dozen Redstone personnel here, and that was, in efficiency, training, brains and dedication, worth a force three times their size. And, Draven acknowledged wryly, if he ordered them to leave, even for their own safety, for one of the very few times in his life he wasn't sure his orders would be followed.

Brown Shirt towered over Tess. She feigned fear and backed up, coming up against a bench seat and sitting down as if she'd lost her balance. Josh knew she was feigning it, because Tessa Marqueza Machado feared nothing. As she'd once said, the worst had already been done to her, so what was left to fear?

"Where the hell is your boss?" Brown Shirt demanded.

Well now, Josh thought, *isn't he supposed to be your boss, too?*

The mild amusement faded quickly, replaced by concern that the man was creeping closer and closer to an unwanted explosion.

"How on earth should I know?" Tess managed to put a

suitably tremulous tone in her voice. "Do you really think he checks in with me?"

"Were you just supposed to sit here and wait around all day?"

"If necessary."

Brown Shirt swore then.

"There's too much going on around here. I thought this was supposed to be a quiet airport."

Sensing the man was on the edge, Josh spoke as if he observed nothing out of the ordinary.

"But it is an airport. And a weekend. We get lots of hikers and hunters coming in." Josh added a shrug for effect. "Maybe we should go have lunch."

The mundane suggestion seemed to startle both Brown Shirt and Pinky.

"I'll put it on Redstone's bill," Josh added, netting him a grin from Pinky. But not from Brown Shirt, who clearly was calling the shots.

And Josh sincerely hoped that wasn't a literal description. He didn't want any of his people hurt. And he knew they were gathering; he'd seen the small jet touch down on the far runway a while ago, telling him even Mac was here.

Any injury sustained by a member of the Redstone family hurt him in a personal way.

And if anything happened to Tess…

He couldn't even complete the thought.

Instead, he made himself focus on what was likely happening outside. St. John's presence had been surprising only at first glance; Dam had a logistical and tactical mind that any commander would be a fool to overlook, and Draven was certainly no fool. And he knew from first-hand experience that his right-hand man was, when motivated, nearly impossible to say no to.

The problem here, Josh thought, was that he himself wasn't used to dealing with this kind of life-or-death situation. Give him a design problem to solve, or a cloud pattern to read or a concept to imagine into reality, that he could do. He could even hunt down dinner if he had to. But animals were predictable, most of the time. Their instincts drove them consistently in one direction—survival.

People, on the other hand, were driven by many other things, and their unpredictability made them the most dangerous creature on the planet. The most wondrous, too, of course, but the most dangerous. Capable of the extremes on both ends of the scale—good and evil.

And despite the actions of these two, he wasn't sure exactly where they fell on that scale. And until he was sure, until he knew their motive, he couldn't make that assessment. But he was also aware the best weapon he and Tess had just now was their ignorance that their prey was actually in their clutches right now. He just had to figure out how to use that to get them out of this.

He had no doubt that Draven had gotten the message they'd been sending. The problem was how to make sure they weren't at cross purposes. The Redstone team had firepower and numbers on their side, but Draven was a firm believer that all-out warfare represented a failure of tactics. He wasn't against doing what he had to, but the phrase "surgical strike" had been invented for men like Draven.

"Unless you've got time and people to waste, don't spend time on the coils, go straight for the head of the snake," he'd told Josh when they'd been about to pull Mac out of the hands of a jungle warlord.

But if you don't know who or where the head is, Josh thought, what then? Waiting was serving for the moment, but his own patience was going to run out soon.

"Maybe the pilot knows where he is, why he's late," Pinky suggested.

Brown Shirt turned to look at his partner, as if startled by the logic of his words. Josh was reminded of the old joke about even a stopped clock being right twice a day; this was number three for Pinky.

And it was the first real chance they'd gotten at taking a step toward ending this.

"Call him," Josh suggested with a shrug, not even looking at either of the men, as if he were intent on his paperwork, which now consisted mainly of a list of parts that had nothing whatsoever to do with the shredded cable. "He's probably in what's laughingly called the lounge inside the terminal building."

For an interminable moment Brown Shirt didn't move. Josh could almost feel him turning over the idea in his mind. Brown Shirt obviously knew that the "pilot" would know he didn't work for Redstone, and had no business being on this plane.

What he didn't know was that with Redstone Security tuned into their every word and move, a golden door had just been opened.

"You," Brown Shirt said suddenly, gesturing at Tess. "You have a way to call the pilot?"

Josh held his breath. He didn't have to; Tess picked up the opportunity without a second's hesitation.

"I have his number on my cell," she said.

"Get your phone."

Josh flicked a glance at the darkened monitor in front of where he sat. The tiny blue light still glowed among the row of yellow and green lights, telling him the webcam and audio connections were still live. He went back to writing on his sham repair order, but this time in larger letters across the top.

Tess went to the cabinet where her combination briefcase and purse had been safely out of sight, a utilitarian piece that managed to look feminine at the same time. They couldn't have known it was there or they would have confiscated her phone. He held his breath for a moment, knowing there had to be things in there that could betray who she really was. And he wanted these two to continue thinking she was unimportant, not worth their attention.

As the two men again watched her, Josh shifted the paper he'd been writing on to where he was fairly sure the wide angle camera lens could pick it up.

"Look up the number," Brown Shirt said to Tess when she had the custom-built Redstone phone in her hand. "You'll make the call, he won't know us." He flicked a glance at "Michael" and added, "Since we just got here and we haven't met yet."

Josh didn't look up, but registered that they were still troubling to keep up the front of being Redstone with him. He said with a creditable laugh, "Didn't have to suffer through that landing, huh?" and kept writing.

And thinking. Brown Shirt had no idea of that phone's capabilities, or he never would have let her near it, Josh thought. She appeared to be fumbling with it, but Josh knew better. His Tess was quick and smart, and he was willing to bet that within seconds she had activated the two-way talk function which would give anyone else with the same phone—which was the entire Redstone Security team—mobile ability to monitor anything said in the same room with the phone, giving them full audio coverage beyond that of the video being streamed from the stationary mics and webcams.

Bless you both, Ian and Ryan, Josh thought; the partnering of Ian Gamble's inventive imagination and Ryan Barton's technical expertise was a match made in progress heaven. He could just picture what was happening outside, hands grabbing for their own phones to mute the receivers on their end; the last thing they needed was for an inadvertent sound or voice to give them away.

Tess held the phone awkwardly for a moment, as if she was having trouble remembering how to call up the number on the complex device. Josh realized what she had done in the moment when she returned the phone to a normal position; she had, brazenly, taken a picture of Brown Shirt as he stood barely eighteen inches away from her. Thanks to Ryan's design, with the camera mounted on the leading edge of the phone instead of on the front or back as almost all others were, Josh doubted the men had any clue what she'd just done.

He had to smother a grin at her nerve; she'd have a portrait-quality shot of Pinky before she was done, too. And she'd have them off to Draven without these two realizing a thing.

"There it is," she said, a bit loudly. To Brown Shirt, Josh guessed she merely sounded nervous. But he knew she simply wanted to be sure her words were clear on the other end. "Right there, under D."

That simply—in a way that Brown Shirt could never guess—she had warned them whose phone was about to ring.

And suddenly Josh was filled with an odd sort of exhilaration. He'd been chained to a desk and paperwork for so long, his only challenges fending off predators in both private and government garb, spending too much precious time in just keeping Redstone free of the pernicious, creeping cancer that was strangling too many others, friends and competitors alike.

He hadn't been in a good, clean fight in a long time.

Too long.

And now that he was, there wasn't anyone he would rather have at his side than the indomitable, courageous, and utterly cool-under-fire Tess Machado.

And there wasn't anyone he would give up more to keep safe.

Chapter 12

When his phone rang, Draven was ready. He answered simply "Hello," instead of his usual, clipped "Draven," not knowing how Tess might have him in her phone.

"John? This is Tess, aboard the Hawk V."

Her voice was amazingly cool, calm and casual. You would never guess there was an armed man leaning over her, close enough to hear the conversation, ordering her to say exactly what he told her to say, as they'd seen on the webcam seconds ago. It was silent now; the moment his phone rang Ryan had put headphones on, muting the sound from the live feed so it didn't come across on the phone connection. At the same time Draven had put the call on speaker, to save time explaining.

He'd only had a minute or two to decide how to play it, and in the end simply went with his gut. "Yeah?" he said, injecting as much impatient annoyance into his voice as he could. Every eye of the team was fastened on him.

"I'm sorry to bother you," Tess said deferentially, "but do you have any idea when Mr. Redstone will be arriving?"

"What's it to you? He's the boss, he can get here whenever he wants."

He intentionally mirrored the tone of the man beside her, peremptory, dictatorial. Ironic, he thought, how so many who decried their supposedly tyrannical bosses turned into exactly what they said they despised when given a little power of their own.

"I just…I mean…." Tess stammered in a way that was totally unlike her, and Draven marveled at the completeness of the picture of helplessness she was projecting to their captors. Wait, Draven thought, until you find out that she's, in fact, the toughest woman you've ever come across.

"Besides, isn't Mike there to fix something?"

"I… Yes."

"He takes his own sweet time, anyway. Right to the edge of your patience," he added, knowing Tess would get the message that that was exactly what they were going to do, push these guys to the edge. It would be a fine line to push them to, not over and into doing something stupid. "So what are you worried about?" he asked.

The man leaned over and spoke to her. Draven caught a clearer look at the man's weapon and grimly added the presence of the boxy, lethal Mac 10 into the mix. As the man straightened up, Draven looked at Ryan, who made quick notes and held up his pad for him to see.

"I just wondered when I should start fixing food for you," she said, matching Ryan's notes of what the man had told her to say in a voice so meek it almost made Draven smile.

As if her tone and subservient question had mollified him, he said grudgingly, "It'll be a while yet. He's waiting for a friend. Be sure and have that lobster stuff he likes ready."

"Shit, he's bringing someone with him?" Pinky said from across the room, loudly enough that Draven didn't need the transcription from Ryan, and confirming his assessment that the smaller man was none too bright.

"It will be ready," Tess said. "We have three of the four ingredients, and I think that will be enough if I can't find the last one."

Draven, his eyes fastened on the video feed, saw the tall man say something to her in the same moment he heard a suppressed muttering over the phone.

"I have to go," Tess said.

"Calm down. I told you it'd be a while."

"My calm is wearing thin," Tess said.

The call went dead abruptly as the tall man grabbed the phone from her. At Draven's nod Ryan unplugged the headphones and removed them.

"—of a bitch!"

The tall man, Draven observed dispassionately, was not happy.

"Mr. Draven?"

Ryan's voice was tentative, although he seemed a bit more at ease since the arrival of the other people not on the security team.

"What is it, Barton?"

"There's something else. Look."

Draven crossed the cabin of the Hawk III and leaned over to look at the monitor. He saw the page where Josh had been writing a list of part numbers and descriptions, some of which had even made them all chuckle; he'd truly like to know what a disgronificator was. But now he saw there was something else in larger, bolder letters, written across the top of the page that had been left just inside the camera's wide-angle view. But with the feeds from all the webcams going, it was still too small to read.

"Can you magnify it?"

"Already did," Ryan said, and held up his own notepad.

The ignorance of one is opportunity for the other.

Slowly, Draven's mouth curved into a smile he was barely aware of. And only belatedly did he realize he was nodding.

"What is it?" Reeve asked.

"Something Josh's brother used to say when going up against an enemy who didn't do his homework," Draven said softly. Then, straightening, he looked at the others. "They're armed now. They know we're here. They'll be ready whenever we are."

"What did Tess tell you?" Grace asked, obviously aware more had been relayed in that phone call than she realized, some additional meaning in the seemingly innocent words.

"They have three of the weapons," Alvera said.

"And we're right, they're losing their cool," Reeve put in. "That bit about calm wearing thin."

Sam said nothing, merely went about checking her gear; Draven knew she hadn't missed the food reference.

"And the lobster," Ian explained quietly, "means one of the people coming for them will be Samantha. She loves the stuff, and Josh knows it."

Draven had expected him to get it; not much got past Ian, despite his sometimes distracted air. Some men might be uncomfortable about it, but he knew the unlikely couple had long ago reached an accord on their vastly divergent careers. Ian had complete and utter faith in his wife's skills, and merely nodded when Draven glanced his way.

Besides, this was Josh, and Draven knew there wasn't a soul at Redstone who wouldn't give anything to get him back safe and sound.

"All right, people," he said, turning the aerial photograph Barton had pulled and routed to the wide-screen television in the main cabin of the Hawk III. He gestured to his wife, the airport builder, to join them, wanting her input. "Let's lay it out. I want any and all ideas."

"What the hell is this supposed to mean?"

Josh saw Brown Shirt holding his list of parts, but knew he was staring at the words written across the top. The man was no longer trying to conceal his foul mood. Or, Josh noted with more concern, the pistol that was now in his hand most of the time.

"Just something my big brother used to say," he answered easily. "He always believed you should do your homework thoroughly before you took action."

Brown Shirt frowned. Josh could almost feel him searching for the possible insult. Yet as far as he knew, it couldn't be, because the mechanic had no idea what was going on. Or so he thought.

"It's business," he said before Brown Shirt could decide it meant something nefarious. "Redstone doesn't know how to repair this plane, I do. Opportunity for me."

Brown Shirt's expression cleared. "So you meant his ignorance. Redstone's."

"Who else?" Josh said with a smile. It was an effort; he was getting mightily tired of playing this game.

In the meantime, his mind was racing, trying to guess what Draven would do. Obviously, he was going to wait for an opportunity; that came through in the patience comment. The lobster remark meant Sam would be coming in, and while the use of the new mother didn't please him, he knew, too, that she was one of the best they had, and her looks were a distraction to any man breathing. She stunned most men into immobility for at least a few seconds.

And frankly, he was glad it wasn't Reeve; the woman had already taken a bullet for him once, and he doubted Zach would appreciate a rerun of that.

Brown Shirt suddenly chirped. All heads turned toward him as he swore and dug a cheap, throwaway-style phone out of his pocket. He flipped it open and pushed a couple of buttons, apparently retrieving a text message.

The string of curses he let out then took even Josh—who'd spent some time in some pretty rough-and-tumble places in his life—aback.

"Nice language," Tess said, earning her a glare.

"Problem?" Josh asked mildly.

"What was that?" Pinky asked. "Nobody's got that number but—"

"Shut up!"

Brown Shirt had apparently reached his limit. Too bad, Josh thought, if he'd been a hair slower to shut up his partner, they might know who was behind all this.

The hapless Pinky tried again. "But what—"

"I said shut up," Brown Shirt roared.

He whirled, and Josh sensed immediately the entire game had shifted. His instincts proved right when the man gestured at them with the distinctively square pistol.

"You two," he said sharply, "get in the back. You—" he turned on Pinky "—stay at the door and keep them there. I need to think."

For an instant Josh thought about resisting. He could bring this thing to a halt one way or another right now, and the idea was very tempting. But Pinky was looking suddenly very nervous, and he was too close to Tess, his own pistol now drawn.

Tess was looking at him, waiting for his lead. And he knew suddenly that if he decided to start a pitched battle right here and now, she'd be with him without question. And he couldn't describe how that made him feel.

"Wait a minute," he said, ostensibly to Brown Shirt, but he knew Tess would understand. "What's going on?"

"Just get back there," Brown Shirt instructed. "Redstone's orders."

"Why would he do that?" Josh asked, figuring at least some question was called for; going along too easily would be suspicious.

"We have private Redstone business to discuss," Brown Shirt said, his voice decisive now, as if he'd decided what tack to take.

"Hey," Pinky said, "what are you complaining about? We're going to put you two alone in a room with a bed."

Tess colored, surprising Josh. Flying was still largely a world of men, and she'd taken much worse than Pinky's comment and rude leer without turning a hair.

"You think I haven't seen the way you two look at each other? Electric, man. Not," he said to Josh, "that I can blame you. I'd like a piece of that hot Latina ass myself."

Tess said something in Spanish, and while Josh didn't quite catch it all—something about Pinky's mother—he was certain the words didn't match the sweetness of her tone.

Josh allowed it to appear that he'd been distracted from his questions. He'd go along for the moment, as if he believed Brown Shirt, although from any sane point of view it was ridiculous. At the same time he was weighing their options. He couldn't quite believe that Brown Shirt would expect the unknowing mechanic to simply obey such an order, but whatever that text message had been—from the person behind all this?—it had clearly rattled him.

And now they were going to put him alone in a room with the woman who actually knew what was going on.

Maybe he just didn't care anymore that the mechanic remain unknowing.

Now there was an unsettling thought to add to the other that had been bothering him all along. Because there was no getting around the one basic, unignorable fact.

No masks.

These guys had let two witnesses see their faces, made no effort to disguise themselves. There was no way that boded well.

Chapter 13

"We wait?" Tess asked softly from the far corner of the stateroom, well away from the door where Pinky hovered. Listening, no doubt, she thought, hoping to hear….

Her mind shied away from that as she watched Josh walk toward the side of the bed that took up a good portion of the stateroom's footprint.

"Draven's here," he answered just as quietly, as if that said it all. As, she supposed, it did.

"Just as well we're in here," she said. "I wouldn't want to be at close range when Brown Shirt finally snaps. Or Pinky drives him over the edge."

"Interesting pair," Josh said, already removing the panel that concealed the compartment built into the side frame of the bed Pinky had leered over. Tess knew she'd blushed at his inference, but she'd fought it down, thinking that of course they'd been looking at each other, trying to communicate without betraying anything to their captors.

Within seconds he had the ACP .45 in his hands. The big

Colt was the largest caliber of all the secreted weapons; it would tear up the plane, but she knew he'd use it if he had to. He walked back to where Tess was, as far as they could get from the door, and she knew he also suspected Pinky was doing his best to eavesdrop. With anyone else she'd assume the guy wanted to hear what they were saying. With Pinky, she had the nasty feeling he was hoping for something more titillating.

"This room isn't monitored," he said, as if simply imparting useful information.

"I know," she said.

Josh gave her a sideways look. "As many flights as you've done that ended up in Redstone weddings, I guess you do."

"You'd make a heck of a matchmaker," she said.

He looked disconcerted. "It's not me. It's like you've always said, if you bring people with the same standards and drive and vision together, it's bound to happen."

"And who is it that brings them together?" His mouth quirked wryly, and despite the situation, her voice was light as she spread her hands and said, "I rest my case."

I only wish it would work for you, she thought, as she always did when the subject came up. It was a measure, she supposed, of how deep her feelings for this man truly were, that she wished he would find happiness, true happiness as he'd had with Elizabeth, with…someone. Even if it wasn't her.

That if he did she would trudge on full of silly, unrequited love would be a small price to pay to see Josh happy again. Although she didn't know if she could bear to fly him and whoever the impossibly lucky woman was all over.

An image flashed through her mind—a sweet memory, pure, true, golden, of the day she'd flown on a Hawk jet for the first time.

"You designed this plane?" she'd demanded the moment they'd touched down.

Josh had nodded.

"Yourself. No team, no subcontractors, just you?"

"I had some advice, suggestions. Took some, ignored more. But the credit or the blame is mine."

"I'll fly for you until they pull my license when I'm eighty."

Josh had merely lifted a brow and drawled, "I was hoping for ninety-five."

"Done," she'd quipped.

Elizabeth had sealed the bargain with a toast, her laughter genuine and true, her warm brown eyes sparkling as much as the champagne in the glass she'd raised.

"Leftover from the launch," she had confessed with no visible embarrassment. "We're not to where we can be profligate. Yet," she added, with a look that had made her husband grin, giddy with the power of her faith in him.

Funny, Tess thought, it hadn't bothered her at all to fly Josh and Elizabeth anywhere they wanted to go, even knowing Josh wasn't flying himself so they could steal some precious time alone together.

But the idea of some new, faceless woman, someone he perhaps had yet to meet, bothered her.

"Tess?"

She snapped back to the present; what a time to be slipping into memories.

"Sorry," she muttered, still keeping her voice barely above a whisper as he had, in case Pinky hadn't gotten bored yet.

"You were far away."

"Only in time," she said.

"What?"

"Elizabeth."

That made him go still. After a moment he said, with no small amount of fervency, "She adored you from the moment she met you. She called you the sister she should have been born with."

"It was mutual."

"I know." Something odd flickered in those gray eyes she knew so well. "She'd want us to remember the good times."

"I was. The day I first flew in a Hawk."

She saw the memory flash through his mind as if it were a video. "Yes," he said softly, "a very good time."

"You know I loved her?" Tess said; it suddenly seemed urgent to be clear.

"And she you. She trusted you with everything."

Somehow I don't think that includes you, Tess thought, then tamped down her unruly mind. It had to be the situation; while she wasn't panicked, there was very clearly danger here. That had to be why her usually disciplined thought process was bucking out of control.

That she'd flown through enemy gunfire and not even blinked was something she couldn't reconcile with her current state of mind.

She couldn't take any more of this. Briskly she asked, "What do you suppose the text message was?"

"I don't know, but it certainly rattled him."

"And he was already on edge."

"Smart enough to be."

"Unlike Pinky," Tess agreed. "He's definitely the follower."

Josh nodded. "But who's the leader? I'm thinking it's not Brown Shirt."

"Almost by definition," she muttered, and saw a brief smile curve his mouth. "So the brains, such as they are, sent the message?"

"Makes sense. What else would perturb him like that?"

"Another colleague with bad news? Somebody else not doing their part?"

"Possible," Josh agreed.

"But from his reaction, you think it's the boss."

He nodded. And given his track record of reading people

in high-power situations, she wasn't about to doubt his assessment.

"Do you think he knows you're you?"

He shook his head. "I think Brown Shirt would have been as much embarrassed as angry if that were the case."

"As well he should be. Not that I'm not thankful, but please," she muttered. At Josh's glance, she smiled ruefully. "I know, I'm spoiled."

"You? Hardly."

"I mean, by Redstone. I'm used to efficiency, competency, thoroughness and sometimes I forget the rest of the world doesn't run to our standards."

The smile he gave her then warmed her. "Thank you."

She gave a one-shouldered shrug. "You know that's true, you don't need me to tell you."

"Yes, I do. Because it means more from you."

That simply took her breath away all over again. And her rationalization that he meant it only as longtime friend and boss was beginning to get a little threadbare.

She made herself move on. "Now what? He kept my phone."

"I know. The two-way is still on?"

She nodded. "I locked it in place."

"Good. If he keeps it on him, Draven will hear everything they say, even if they're out of range of the webcam mics."

Tess gave a wry shake of her head. "Draven must love this. Of all the things we planned for, kidnappers who don't even recognize you wasn't on the list."

"You've always said I looked like a mountain man when I come back from these treks."

"You do," she said. "But more important, you look happy. At least, you usually do. This time not so much, even before you saw those clowns. Odell?"

His mouth twisted. "Yeah, well. Time enough for that grim tale later. Now, we have a problem to deal with."

"Did I get that right?" she asked, lowering her voice even more, although there was no way Pinky could hear anything lower than a raised voice through the solidly built bulkhead and tightly sealed door. "Draven's going to wait until he thinks they're about to snap, and then Sam and…somebody will be coming in?"

"That's how I interpreted it."

"So what do we do?" She looked around. "Try and barricade ourselves in here? It's not like we can climb out a window."

"Makes me reconsider Draven's request for an escape hatch," Josh said dryly. "I said no way at the time because it would affect the integrity of the design."

"He's rarely wrong," Tess said.

"But I'm guessing he's feeling pretty irritated with himself about now for not anticipating something like this."

"Who could? I mean, it's insanely stupid to not study your target inside and out, let alone not even recognize him in mountain-man mode or not."

"Unless," Josh said, "they didn't have time."

"So you think this was just some kind of impulse thing? They saw the plane, decided the owner had to be worth something?"

"Maybe. Or maybe it's somebody else's plan put together in a big hurry. Either way, it doesn't change what we have to do."

"Which is?"

"Prepare the best we can. And then wait."

She grimaced. And then, unexpectedly, Josh was smiling at her.

"Ah, Tess, waiting has never been your strong suit, has it?"

I've been learning, ever since I realized what an idiot I am, she thought. His gaze sharpened, and for an instant she was afraid she'd spoken aloud.

"Tess?"

"You don't want to know," she muttered. "Trust me."

"I do trust you. Implicitly."

She wasn't unaware of the honor of that, despite the fact that it wasn't his trust she wanted. But it was what she had. It was worth more from him than anyone else in the world, and she treasured it.

"So what do we do to prepare? We have the guns, what else can we do?"

"Short of locking ourselves in the head?" She knew the grin was to cheer her.

"Speaking of locks," she asked, "do you think they even realize this room has a lock on the door, only on this side?"

"Hope not," Josh said.

"So if somebody tries to break through that door, we'll know it's them?"

"I'm assuming John or Sam will simply announce themselves," he said, that grin flashing again.

"You," she said with sudden understanding, "are enjoying this."

"To a certain extent, and except for worrying about you getting hurt, yes, I am."

"Don't worry about me."

He stopped then, turning to look at her directly. "Sorry. Not possible. For so many reasons."

That took her aback. "What?"

"You're one of my oldest and dearest friends. You're one of the triumvirate. You're my right hand as much as St. John is, sometimes more. You're Elizabeth's sister by choice. But most of all, you're Tess. So obviously, I worry."

Tess simply stared at him. He'd said all those things at one time or another, but never all at once. And never with that odd sort of emphasis on "you're Tess." She told herself to stop reading her wishes into places they didn't belong or fit.

"Besides," he added, his voice going even softer, "Elizabeth ordered me to."

Tess felt an odd combination of chill and heat. "She... what?"

"When...she knew it wouldn't be long, she told me to always look out for you. I mean, I would have because you're you, but I promised her."

The chill was winning. She looked away, looked out through the oval porthole window of the cabin, which was larger than most thanks to another Ian Gamble bit of genius—a plastic polymer that was as strong as the metal around it. It was time, past time, to face the fact she should have accepted long ago, that she would ever and always be connected to Elizabeth in his mind, and therefore as untouchable as if that sisterhood of the heart had been of blood.

"You worry about me simply because Elizabeth asked you to?" she whispered.

"There's nothing simple about it. You know there's more to it than just that, Tess. Besides, she said you'd look out for me, too. And you have."

Tess didn't know how to feel, let alone how to respond.

"She actually said that?"

He nodded. Then frowned slightly. "And that she trusted us to find our way."

Tess's heart gave a funny jump. "Find our way?"

"Without her, I guess," Josh said, sounding puzzled.

"Or to something?"

Even as she said it Tess was silently lecturing herself about reading anything beyond friendship in a dead woman's words. However much Elizabeth Redstone might have liked—even loved—her, that didn't mean she'd meant to hand off her husband to her when she knew her time was running out.

"So," she said hastily, "we just wait for them to do something?" She was beyond caring that her change of subject was both obvious and embarrassed.

"Which them?" Josh asked, accepting the diversion. Or, Tess thought wryly, more likely not even realizing the need for one. Just because her mind had veered into dangerous territory—again—didn't mean his had.

"Either them," she said. "Either Draven makes a move, or these guys do something really stupid."

"My money's on selection B," Josh said.

"If they were smart, the way you look now wouldn't be enough," Tess said.

"Question is, should we be glad they're not smart, or worried?"

Tess's mouth quirked. "Yes," she said.

Josh grinned. "Ah, Tess, I do love the way you think."

And I love you, she thought.

And wondered if she'd die before she ever said that to him out loud.

Chapter 14

We're going to put you two alone in a room with a bed.

He'd be thinking a lot clearer if Pinky's words would stop echoing in his head, Josh thought.

And if those words hadn't gotten him to thinking in directions he had no business going. This was Tess, Elizabeth's adopted sister. The woman he'd promised Eric Machado he would take care of, should anything happen to him. And he'd made that promise knowing that, given Eric's chosen career, having to keep it was a very real possibility.

Not that he would have needed a promise to do it; Tess was Redstone; that alone would be enough. But he hadn't been flattering her when he'd said she was his right hand as much as St. John. It was true; he relied on her common sense and wisdom and wit, in some ways even more than the once dour, laconic St. John.

And he admired her. Tremendously. Once she'd accepted his job offer, she'd applied herself with an industry that had, in fact, set the standard for all Redstone people who would follow. She'd added her twin engine, instrument and jet ratings so fast that everything had been questioned and double-checked in disbelief. To this day, she was the best sale-closing tool Redstone Aviation had; one flight with her at the controls for one of her trademark featherlight landings, and the customer was ready to sign.

But it wasn't just her prodigious flying skills he admired; it was Tess herself. Her generally cheerful outlook despite her share of life's travails, her attitude and a devotion to Redstone and its people that rivaled his own. He'd long ago lost track of how many times she had uncomplainingly changed her own plans because someone needed her, how many times she had flown Redstone personnel to where they needed to be for reasons professional or often personal.

And when those personal reasons were grim or painful, Tess was unfailingly compassionate and kind, and he inevitably heard back that she had been a rock in a difficult time.

"The only good thing I can see about going through that," she'd told him one day long after they'd buried her husband and handed her the flag that had draped his casket, "is that it helps you understand how to help when others go through it."

In that instant, he regretted letting his mind slip back to those long-ago days. Because in the next instant, the memory that followed that one hit him; Tess stretching up on tiptoe to give him a grateful kiss. He'd never forgotten that moment, if for no other reason than the startling inappropriateness of his response.

He loved Tess like the sister she'd been to Elizabeth, which certainly didn't include feeling the first jolt of physical attraction since Elizabeth. He knew many said he'd buried his heart with her, and for a very long time he'd thought that true. He'd placed himself in the ranks of the walking wounded—those who had lost a large piece of their heart and soul who kept on living because they didn't know what else to do, because they'd survived beyond the initial urge to follow that chunk of themselves into the grave it had been consigned to along with the shell of the one who had held that heart and soul.

There had been times, once the grief had ebbed to a constant but dull pain, when meeting a woman had sent a faint spark of interest through him. But it had always died before he'd summoned up the energy to pursue it. Never had it been strong enough to overcome the memories of what he'd once had, strong enough to quash the sense of betrayal the very idea of being with someone else gave him.

He knew that there were many who would be glad to see him with someone, others who had actively worked toward that goal, searching out women they thought might interest him. And when whatever it was had gotten into the Redstone water in the past few years, and started the cascade of matchings that had resulted in so many engagements and marriages, he'd gone beyond being bemused to being amazed. He knew it had come with that seemingly inevitable accompaniment; the urge of the newly in love to see everyone around them in the same state.

"Draven will never let anything happen to you."

Tess's words yanked him out of the reverie, and he wryly told himself to focus on the matter at hand or even Draven might not be able to keep that vow.

"I wasn't worried about it," he said.

"You looked…preoccupied."

"I was," he said, "but not about that."

And he wasn't about to admit to her what memory loop he'd been caught up in.

"It's hard to just wait," she said.

"I know."

Not that she had been, he thought; she'd been moving about the cabin, searching for anything else that could possibly be used as a weapon. She'd given him one of a couple of razor blades from the head—useful, he supposed, if they ended up tied up—and was hefting a letter opener from the small desk.

"Harder for me," she added, giving him a sideways look. "You have a lot more patience."

"Tweedledee and Tweedledum out there are running through my patience in a big hurry."

She raised a brow at him. "Then, if we see a chance…?"

"We take it," he confirmed, deciding in that moment. "I'd just as soon Draven not have to risk any of the team."

Tess smiled at that. "That's their job. You know that's what he'd say."

"Yes. But we're already in this, we have no choice. If we could end this now…"

"Part of my job is to not let you risk yourself," she said.

He'd always suspected Draven had thoroughly indoctrinated her when he'd absconded with her for a month the day after Josh had announced she'd be flying him regularly from then on. Now he knew it.

"You *are* Redstone, no matter how much you like to claim everyone else is. If something happened to you, Redstone as we know it would be over."

He grimaced. "Some," he said sourly, "would like it that way."

"Of course they would. You're a beacon to their enemies, individuals of courage and free spirit," she said, and he was thankful he didn't have to explain. But he never did, not to Tess.

For a moment she looked as if she wanted to say more, but had decided this wasn't the time. And she was right; they should be planning how to take back this plane, not just waiting for rescue. He had never been simply a reactor, nor had she. But he so rarely had time to just talk with her out from under the load of running Redstone. That despite the situation, and the odd undercurrents that seemed to be running between them, he was…not enjoying it, under the circumstances, but at least savoring it.

"Tess," he said suddenly.

She had been searching through a drawer, but stopped and turned to look at him. "What?"

"I… Nothing."

He had, he realized, just wanted to say her name, and hadn't thought beyond that. Such vagueness wasn't something he did, and he felt decidedly and strangely awkward. This was Tess, there was no reason for this odd tangle of emotions.

Except for the fact that there are two not-too-bright guys with guns in the outer cabin.

He supposed that must be it. It was one thing to live with the concept of every human being's mortality; most people past the self-indulgence of their twenties did. It was another to live with the reality of it, as he and Tess did every day.

But it was something quite different to live with the possibility of your own potentially imminent death walking around in the next room.

There had been a time when he would have welcomed it. When he'd ached so much with Elizabeth's loss that the idea of death had been a constant companion, when he'd wished for it to take him, too. Sometimes only the knowledge that he would be letting down everything she'd stood for, betraying every part of himself she had so completely believed in, had stopped him from taking one of the Hawks up and cratering it into the side of a mountain.

"We'll get out of this, Josh," she said, and it took him a moment to realize she was responding to his uncustomary stammering. She thought he was worried about their situation, and he was. But the urge to simply say her name hadn't had anything to do with that.

"I know we will," he said. "If I've descended to the point where two clowns like that can take me out, then I should just give up now."

"You? Never. You're Josh Redstone. You always will be."
Her faith in you is endless....

Eric's words, spoken at their wedding, echoed in Josh's head. Her husband had been quiet, steady, and utterly unthreatened by his new wife's devotion to her job and her boss. He had the same sort of steely strength leavened with innate goodness that his own brother had had, and Josh had liked him immediately.

And the night after his funeral, Josh had gone to the house Eric and Tess had shared so joyously on his rotations home.

"I know the path you're on," he had told her, refusing to let her send him away. "It twists and turns, and at the fork I know where it can lead. I'll be here until you're headed in the direction Eric would have wanted."

"What on earth are you thinking?" Tess asked now, telling him he'd been too deeply lost in memory once more. Another thing he didn't make a habit of, and another thing he'd best be watching out for if they were going to get out of this unharmed.

"Eric," he said succinctly, as she had earlier simply said "Elizabeth."

"Oh." Her voice was small, almost deflated, as unlike her as stammering had been unlike him.

"I promised him, too," he said.

"I can take care of myself." Her tone had shifted, sounding a bit acerbic now.

"You surely can. And I don't envy the man or woman who thinks otherwise."

"I don't need looking out for," she said, but she sounded at least a little mollified.

"Right now," he said, "I think we both do. We've always looked out for each other, haven't we?"

And then she was Tess again, his Tess. "Yes, we have. And we always will. No matter what."

Chapter 15

"What in the hell are they after?" Noah Rider paced the Hawk III cabin, staring at the video feed at every sharp turn he made to come back toward the gathered group.

"We have no way of knowing since in their view, they don't have their quarry," Reeve said, her words reasonable in contrast to her voice, which sounded as if she wanted to swear just as Rider had.

The two glanced at Draven. "Fine line you're walking," Rider said.

"I know."

"No guarantee what they'll do when they run out of patience," Alvera said.

"None," Draven agreed, eyes fixed on the monitor showing the video feed from the Hawk V.

For a moment, no one said anything. Then, almost uncertainly, Ryan Barton turned to look over his shoulder at Draven.

"Sir? I've been thinking..." He stopped, hesitating.

Draven shifted his gaze from the screen to the young tech's face. Barton might not be security, but he'd done everything asked of him and then some. "Go ahead."

"If one of those goofs decides to check out that computer, or tries to boot it up…"

He paused. Draven doubted either of these two would, but he never discarded input out of hand. Especially when it came to computers; he was a good end user, but Barton's knowledge was far, far beyond that. "What?"

"I was thinking if I set up a reverse feed, from here to the system there, we could use it to give them info. You know, whatever we wanted."

Draven blinked.

"I mean," Barton hastened to go on, "we could send them fake weather reports about a storm, fake news reports, make them nervous, that kind of thing."

Draven stared at the young man with the spiky, blond-tipped hair.

"I just thought it might help at some point," Barton said, sounding embarrassed now.

Draven put a hand on Barton's shoulder. "You," he said, "are a credit to Josh's instincts."

Barton's eyes widened, and he flushed slightly. "Thanks," he muttered.

"You can get that ready, just in case?"

"Absolutely!"

Barton went to work immediately on his own sleek, racy-looking laptop, which Draven guessed was probably more powerful than most corporate servers. The rest of them continued to watch the feed.

"You think we can just wait them out?" Alvera asked.

His voice was even, but Draven didn't miss the undertone. He wasn't surprised; he had figured it would be Alvera, ever the man of action, who would chafe first at the waiting.

Or Tess, he thought with an inward smile. She was one for

getting the job done, and now. And she inevitably did it well and with Redstone style.

Now Josh had infinite patience. He was a firm believer in the maxim that if the opposition was in the process of self-destructing, get out of the way and let them do it. Something Draven himself believed in, for the most part.

As long as they don't take you down with them, he thought.

The problem with waiting, besides being frustrating, was that the more time they had, the more chance there was that these two seemingly inept conspirators would tumble to the fact that the man they were waiting for was already there, right under their noses, and had been for some time. Plus, Draven had the feeling they wouldn't take kindly to the revelation; no one hated being shown up as a fool worse than a real fool.

And they were fools; Draven had no doubt of that. What he didn't know was how much of a fool the person pulling the strings was.

And he would give a great deal to know what the text message that had set off the tall man—and that he assumed had come from that string-puller—had said.

"Uh-oh," Sam said suddenly. Draven wheeled around. The tall blonde was looking out a side window of the Hawk III. "The locals…make that local, singular, has arrived."

"Guess the airport manager wasn't completely blinded by your gorgeousness, Sammy," Rand said. The two, who looked enough alike to be assumed siblings, had often been partnered and used the resemblance in their work, and as a result had developed a camaraderie that resulted in the kind of teasing and jabbing actual siblings were prone to.

"Let me deal with this," Draven said, only able to imagine what the reaction of the lone sheriff's deputy who had pulled up would be to the sight of the entire Redstone contingent now gathered. "The rest of you stay put."

"You going to tell him?" Alvera, whose youthful wariness of official uniforms had never quite left him, asked.

"I won't lie to him," Draven said.

"Now, there's a nice evasion," ex-cop Beck said, but he was smiling.

Draven pulled out his phone, last used to receive the two crystal-clear photographs of the armed men Tess had managed to send. He'd sent them in turn to Lilith and Liana, who were tracking down who the two men were.

He called up the name and number he'd picked out of all the ones from the local sheriff's office that Lilith had called him back with, and dialed it.

The exchange with the man who had once worn the same military uniform and patch was friendly, brief and effective; James Redstone had had the same effect on people as his brother, his reputation had been well-known, and the mention of his name was all it had taken.

By the time he was done, the deputy outside was on foot, walking around the big plane. Draven headed for the rear hatch they'd opened to enable them quick entrance and exit, yet keep the main door secured. The rear one could be closed in motion if necessary; it was an old habit he'd never tried to break.

The deputy was young, and in the moments before he put on his official face, Draven caught the look of awed surprise as he stared at the Hawk III. Probably didn't see planes this size here often, if ever.

Might be seeing a lot of this one, he thought as he walked across the tarmac, *since we may never get it out of here.*

The deputy eyed him warily, but without fear or any move toward his sidearm, Draven noted. He knew he had only a short time to decide how far to trust the man, but he'd made a career out of quickly and accurately assessing people.

"Gary there," the deputy, whose name tag labeled him as R. Lockner, said, jabbing a thumb back toward the single airport building, "says you're Redstone. That true?"

"It is." He studied the eyes that looked back at him, saw that wariness still, but no fear, and more important no recklessness or macho bravado. "But then, since I'm sure you've run the tail number, you already know that."

The flicker of a smile that crossed the young man's face told him he'd judged well. And the assessing look the deputy gave him told him he was doing some measuring of his own.

"Heard of you guys. Redstone Security, I mean."

Draven liked that he didn't ask. The intelligence in his eyes told him the man probably knew he wouldn't answer directly anyway.

"All good," the deputy said, "even the bad stuff."

It sounded nonsensical, but Draven knew exactly what he meant; Redstone Security's reputation for getting the job done rested in part on their freedom, and that freedom was envied by many in the much more rigid world of government-controlled law enforcement.

Lockner's cell phone rang. Draven nodded. "I'll wait," he said, and adopted a relaxed posture with arms folded across his chest to tacitly underline he was no threat to the deputy. Besides, he knew what the call would be.

"Lockner." Surprise crossed the man's face. "Yes, sir. Out at the airport."

There was a pause on this end as the deputy listened; Draven guessed he was wondering why he was getting a call from the captain of detectives when he was in uniformed patrol.

"Oh. Okay. Yes, sir, absolutely. I will."

When the call ended and he put away the cell, the deputy looked at him. "You knew that was coming, didn't you?"

Draven didn't dissemble. "Yes."

The man lifted a brow, then nodded, a glint of appreciation for the honesty showing in his eyes. "He said I'm to give you anything you need, and to not give you anything you don't want."

"How do you translate that, Deputy Lockner?"

"Loosely? Hand you my gun if you ask for it, and then get out of your way."

Draven smiled inwardly; he liked this guy. Smart, quick, and no ego to get in the way of getting the job done.

"I have to ask if there's any risk to the locals in why you're here."

Draven understood both the question and the subtle message beneath it; the man would do what he was ordered, but only insofar as it didn't conflict with doing his job, which he saw as protecting the people of his county. Draven respected that. His job, after all, was to protect Redstone in much the same way.

And in that moment he decided to trust the young deputy.

"Any problem will be restricted to this airfield," he said, his gaze flicking toward the slate-gray-and-red Hawk V parked downfield. "But if you could keep the population around here to the minimum, that would give me one less thing to worry about."

"I can keep the population around here to zero, and nobody'd notice much." At Draven's look he explained, "Gary has a habit of putting out a recorded notice on the airport frequency that the landing strip is temporarily closed when he wants a long lunch. I'll go tell him he's hungry."

The smile broke through to the outside this time. "You ever get tired of the public trough, you call me," Draven said.

"I just might someday," Lockner said. "Redstone sounds like my kind of place."

"And you might just be Redstone's kind of person," Draven said.

"What will Draven do when he decides to move?" Tess asked.

"The best thing possible," Josh answered.

It wasn't really a helpful answer, specifically, but Tess knew it was the absolute truth. Because that was what Draven always did. That sometimes the best thing possible wasn't very good, such as the trauma he'd had to inflict to save the woman who would become his wife, didn't change that.

"Josh," she said, suddenly filled with a dread unlike anything she'd felt in a very long time.

He turned to look at her. She said nothing more, just as he had uttered only her name a while ago.

"It's going to be okay, Tessie. I promise."

The long ago, almost forgotten nickname—allowed to only two men in the world, Eric and this man—echoed in her ears. She hadn't heard it since Eric had been killed, as if it had been buried with him. Hearing it now, from Josh, stirred her already roiling emotions into chaos.

She wanted more than anything to go to him then. To cross the three feet between them and throw her arms around him. But that yard of distance might as well have been a mile-deep gulf, full of years of memories and grief and friendship and respect and all the things that made what she was wishing so impossible.

And then Josh moved, did what she'd wanted to, covered the yard of space between them in one, long stride. His strong arms enveloped her, and she was suddenly where she'd longed to be.

"It's going to be all right," he said. "We can beat these two with our eyes closed if we have to."

Tess shivered. Josh's arms tightened. She knew it was only to comfort her, knew he meant only to reassure her, but for a moment, just for a moment, she let herself savor it, revel in it. Just for a moment she did something she'd never before allowed herself; she let her thoughts, her fantasies run free, let herself imagine what it would be like.

She let herself because there were two armed men outside, and she might never get the chance again. The reality was as out of her reach as ever, but it would be a shame to die without even having indulged in the fantasy.

She was barely aware that she was hugging him back, and that he was letting her. She knew only that he filled the deep, empty space inside her in a way no one else ever could.

"I don't like not being able to see Josh and Tess," Reeve fretted.

"But at least we know they're safe, and together in one place," Alvera said.

"And probably plotting like mad," Sam said, with a glance at Draven.

He nodded. "We have to take that into account. Neither of them is going to be content to just sit back and wait to be rescued."

"But they'll wait for us to move, won't they?" Beck asked.

"Maybe," Draven said. "Josh has infinite patience, but if a chance arises, or these guys do something that triggers him…"

"He didn't get to where he is by being a pushover," Mac said. "If an opportunity presents itself, he'll take it." His mouth quirked. "For that matter, so will Tess."

"Amen," Noah Rider said, somewhat fervently.

"This is crazy," Brown Shirt said, sounding angry enough that Draven turned around to look at the image on the monitor. "I'm sick of waiting."

The tension in the group ratcheted up a notch as the words echoed from the speakers in the main cabin.

"If they get impatient enough, they might cut their losses and try for what they can get for Tess, and the plane," Rand said, shoving back the stubborn lock of platinum-blond hair that was a perfect match to Sam's long tresses; obviously, he'd gotten all the details on the flight. He'd been up to speed from the get-go.

"I hope not," Beck said quietly.

Something in his voice made them all look at him. Only St. John immediately nodded in understanding.

"Makes the…mechanic expendable."

"He's no use to them then," Draven said, arriving there on St. John's heels. "Maybe even a hindrance."

"We can't give them the time or chance to even think that," Alvera said.

"Agreed," Draven said. "So we give them something else to think about."

"But what?" Reeve asked. "What can we do that'll distract them from the fact that they don't have what they came for?"

"What they came for," Mac said suddenly.

Reeve glanced at him. "What?"

"We give them what they came for."

"You know Josh's rule—"

"I don't mean money."

The others fell silent. They all knew Harlan McClaren was, in his own way, nothing less than a genius, worth listening to on any subject.

"Then what?" Grace asked, gently.

Harlan nodded as if he'd thought through his plan and found it acceptable. He looked at Draven.

"We give them Josh."

Chapter 16

Tess told herself to pull away. She told herself if she stayed, she was going to start reading things into this long embrace that Josh never intended. Then she made it an internal order, and finally managed to step back.

"I—"

Her voice was impossibly tight, and she knew she couldn't trust it not to break. She turned from him, staring unseeingly out the window as if the view of the tiny airfield was fascinating.

"Tess—"

He stopped when she shook her head.

"I'm sorry," he said.

She almost asked him for what, but wasn't sure she wanted to know. She—

Her thoughts broke off as something outside finally registered. Chastising herself for being distracted by such things when they were in a perilous situation, she leaned forward to make sure of what she'd seen.

"There can't be another man here now with hair that color," she murmured, almost to herself.

"What?"

"Rand," she said.

Josh blinked. "But he's up in—"

"He's here. I just saw him go into the terminal building."

Josh walked swiftly across the cabin. "Alone?"

She turned to look at him. "No. With Gabe Taggert."

Josh blinked. "What the hell is Gabe doing here?"

"I was about to ask the same thing about him," she said, pointing at another man who, clad in the overalls of the fuel company whose logo was posted prominently, was busying himself near a fuel truck parked about thirty feet away.

"Noah," Josh said when he saw his premiere point man. But he didn't sound nearly as surprised as when he'd seen Gabe, who at least was ex-navy. Noah Rider, Tess knew, had a reputation for many things: efficiency, details, organization, once globe-trotting for Redstone as few others did until he voluntarily slowed his pace to spend more time with his wife, stepson, Kyle, and to prepare for the imminent arrival of their twins. He hadn't had a reputation for danger until the day he'd been forced to it, when that yet-to-be wife and stepson and a classroom full of children had been taken hostage by drug-running terrorists at the Redstone Bay Resort.

"You're surprised about Gabe, but not Noah?" she asked.

"Noah," he said, glancing at her, "owes you his life."

Startled, she looked at the lean, dark-haired man. He always stirred memories of that day in Colombia when they'd barely made it out of the jungle, the helicopter taking rounds from the drug lord's forces—so many she'd wondered how it stayed aloft. She'd trimmed a few trees in that one; her orders had been not to land, not to touch a skid on Colombian soil, and that's what she'd done, hovering like a juicy target while Noah and John Draven, sent to obtain his release in whatever way necessary, scrambled aboard.

"For that matter," Josh added, "so does Draven."

It was so close to her own thoughts that she blinked, startled. Told herself it was logical that he be thinking of the same thing she'd thought of when he'd mentioned Noah owing her his life.

"Draven got him out of there. All I did was—"

Josh cut her off with a shake of his head. "Don't belittle what you did. It was an incredible piece of flying. Under fire as you were, it was nearly impossible. Those eleven bullet holes you brought that chopper back with prove that. But you did it."

"My job," she said, not knowing what else to say in the face of his effusive praise. "Still sorry for the cost of the damage."

"I would have paid a hell of a lot more to have you back safely."

Tess forgot to breathe for a moment. Told her suddenly racing heart to just calm down. It was the aftereffects of that unexpected embrace; it was messing up her mind.

Of course that had been an all encompassing "you." He'd meant them all, Draven, Noah and her, not just she personally. She meant a lot to him, she knew that, by sheer dint of longevity and shared history, if nothing else.

She didn't know what was showing in her face, but it made him say quietly, "I couldn't do without you, Tess."

Her breath stopped completely then. She stared at him. Wanted to say something, anything. She saw his eyes widen slightly, guessed that this time she had betrayed herself, fool that she was. And that wasn't something she was used to— playing the fool.

"Josh," she whispered.

She barely managed not to reach out to him, wanting his heat, his strength again. For an instant, she thought something different sparked in those familiar gray eyes. Something beyond the usual warmth and appreciation he always gave her. And in that instant his hand moved, as if he were going to reach out to her.

"Hey! They locked the door!"

Pinky's exclamation shattered the moment, and Tess belatedly realized she'd been hearing muffled exchanges between the two men for several seconds before. Tess looked at Josh, realizing with no small amount of shame she should have been planning what they were going to do to get out of this, not dwelling on all that emotional drek.

"Wait," he said. "Draven's team isn't all in place yet, or there would have been a signal."

She nodded.

Then, with the oddest expression she'd seen on his face in all the years she'd known him, Josh Redstone leaned down and kissed her. Quick, but hard, hot and fierce, taking her breath away. For a split second he held her, and she felt his grip tighten, as if he'd somehow sensed the explosion of fire that had shot through her.

Or felt it himself.

His hands slipped upward, his fingers tangled in her hair as he tilted her head back. For an instant he deepened the kiss, and something heavy and molten moved through her when she felt the briefest brush of his tongue over her lips, as if he were tasting her.

The door handle rattled loudly. He released her. She nearly staggered backward. For a moment he stared down at her. Tess felt her heart hammering, hoped what she was feeling wasn't showing in her face. Something hot and alive flickered in Josh's eyes, something she hadn't seen in so long she couldn't remember exactly when or where.

Then, with a cool that would have done his security chief proud, he turned and walked toward the door. And, amazingly, opened it.

"Geez," he said ruefully, looking down at Pinky from his

full six-foot-three, "you practically order me to make a move on her, then you interrupt?"

Pinky looked utterly disconcerted. His gaze flicked to her, and she knew what she must look like, her lips swollen, her hair tousled. He looked her up and down avidly, and she had the definite feeling he was searching for something left unbuttoned. His stare made her skin crawl, even as she realized that had Josh looked at her that way, it would have sparked sensations she'd never felt before.

She knew Josh had done it as cover. Knew it didn't mean… anything. But she barely managed to resist lifting her fingers to her lips, as if somehow she could replicate the feel of his mouth on hers.

"Get her out here," Brown Shirt was ordering from behind Pinky. "I want her to call that pilot again."

Tess sensed Josh tense for a split second. Then, casually, he suggested, "Let me talk to him. I know John, we've had a drink together now and then. Maybe I can get him to tell me more than he'll tell her."

Tess didn't react to his emphasis on the last word, clearly relegating her to the paid-servant class despite the fact that he'd just kissed the stuffing out of her; the persona she was presenting probably wouldn't even realize it. And it continued to play into the obvious perceptions of their two captors.

And Brown Shirt bought it. The glimmer of realization flickered in her mind. She'd wondered how he could think that he could order "Michael" around, shut him up in a guarded room and still think the guy wouldn't get that something huge was wrong.

Because he thinks everyone is stupider than him? she wondered, watching the man as he eyed the supposed mechanic carefully, then finally nodded.

"You got his number?"

Say no, Tess urged silently, knowing if the man saw Josh's phone and paid the slightest bit of attention he could figure it out.

"No," Josh said. "My phone's back in the hangar. Didn't figure I'd have to spend all day on this."

"Tell me about it," Pinky muttered.

"Just give me her phone, and I'll hit redial," Josh said.

In that moment Tess was grateful Brown Shirt had kept her phone instead of either giving it back to her or telling her to put it back in her bag; if he'd gone digging around in there he would have found her pilot's log and her ID—including her pilot's license—and the game would have been up. And she didn't think he'd take kindly to having been fooled so badly.

The man pulled it out of the shirt pocket he'd placed it in. Whatever they'd been discussing before Pinky's shout obviously had been heard by Draven, either over the phone or with the webcam mics. Tess only hoped that with them out of the way, they'd been indiscreet enough to let something helpful slip.

Brown Shirt studied the mechanic for a moment. Josh was giving off a completely believable air of it mattering nothing to him one way or the other. And then, incredibly, as if he'd shared her own thoughts, he lifted a hand to his mouth and rubbed his lips with his thumb, as if remembering the feel of their kiss.

"So was she hot?" Pinky asked, as if she weren't standing right there.

"Incredibly," Josh said softly, but loud enough for her to hear. She didn't try to fight the color that rose in her cheeks, figuring the Tess they thought she was would react in just that way. That she'd never in her life blushed at such things before didn't matter, except to inwardly rattle her a bit.

"In fact," Josh added with a grin that was almost rakish, "I hope you've got some more private business to discuss."

Brown Shirt made a disgusted sound, but he handed over

the phone. "I pushed redial. You just talk," he ordered. "And hold it so I can hear."

"Sure," Josh said easily, as if it all made sense. It suddenly dawned on her that these men thought they could get away with all these arrogant, arbitrary actions and orders because that's how they thought a man at Josh's level worked. No lowly mechanic would question they were who they said they were, because they were, in their minds, acting exactly like someone who worked for the legendary Joshua Redstone would act.

Fools, she thought again. Wrong on so many levels. But it would be, she promised silently, their downfall.

Chapter 17

"Hey, John. Mike here."

Every person back on board the Hawk III froze at the sound of Josh's familiar voice coming through the speakers in the instant before Ryan Barton cut it off by plugging in his headphones again.

Although they all knew he was all right, had all been watching the video feed since their more in-depth recon, Draven guessed that the jab of relief he felt at the direct contact had been felt by all of them.

"Hey," he said. "What's up? Don't tell me you're in a hurry, too."

"Even my patience has limits."

Draven knew that even Josh's celebrated cool would run out eventually. Especially when the situation involved risk to Redstone's own.

"I don't know what Redstone's paying, but it's probably a lot," he said.

As he'd hoped, Josh picked it up quickly. "At this point, I don't know if money is the object."

So Josh and Tess knew nothing more than they did about the motive behind all this.

"Won't know until the man arrives, I suppose," Draven said.

"Get on with it!"

The harshly whispered order from the man standing next to Josh was muffled over the phone, but Barton quickly wrote it out.

"Exactly," Josh said. "No way to know. And I'm tired of waiting around."

"If you worked for Redstone, you'd be used to it. I know all about them."

There was a second's pause before Josh answered, in a quieter tone that told them he'd gotten the message that they'd identified the gunmen.

"Do you, now." It wasn't a question.

"Yes. Small-time with big connections, that's them." And that was about as much as he could risk, he thought, and moved on. "So when exactly do you think you're going to run out of patience?"

He knew Josh would understand he wanted a guess on their captors' breaking point. "Soon," Josh said, adding. "I've got a date with an angel I can't miss."

The angel flight, Draven thought. He glanced over at St. John who nodded, indicating he'd already made arrangements to cover it. Draven had expected no less; no detail ever seemed to escape the man—unless he was distracted by Jessa, which made for enjoyable entertainment for all who had known the taciturn to a fault, haunted man he'd once been.

"Hey, I can handle that for you," he said into the phone. "You just wait long enough, and things work out."

"He'd better make it fast, or I'll just handle it from this end and he'll have to live with it."

And that, Draven thought, *was aimed at me.* "Relax." Then he threw in a tidbit for the man hovering next to Josh. "His friend's already here, so it'll probably only be a little while longer. Go play a computer game."

On the video monitor, he saw Josh's brow furrow for a split second.

"Yeah, sure," Josh muttered.

He was tempted to add a hint to grab Tess and work out whatever the hell was standing in their way, but he didn't think it appropriate at the moment. He studied the man leaning over the phone to eavesdrop, thought maybe one more reassurance might help.

"Tell you what, I'll call you when he gets here," Draven said, in the tone of one magnanimously making an effort to help.

"Thanks," Josh said. Then, after a glance at the man beside him, he added, "I'll hang out awhile longer."

The question was, Draven thought as the connection was abruptly ended when the other man grabbed the phone, would the two hostage takers? If he misjudged this or them, things could go to hell in a big hurry. But Josh had indicated he thought the call and the reassurances had bought them a little more time.

Not that they needed it, he thought as he looked at his team, and all the additional Redstone people who had gathered. They were ready, more than ready; they were nearly as impatient as the gunmen. The difference was they were professional, highly trained and competent. Not to mention critical thinkers; none of them would ever make such a huge blunder out of their own prejudices.

"Barton?" he said.

The young tech genius nodded. "Ready whenever you say."

"As soon as he reactivates it on that end."

Again Barton nodded. His fingers hovered over the

keyboard, ready to strike in the same way any other person on the team would be when the right second arrived.

And in that moment, Draven had never been prouder to be part of Redstone, part of the magnificent thing a young man, barely more than a boy, had built on a single design and a dream.

A computer game.

Draven knew perfectly well that except for the occasional game of chess when he needed to think about tactics and strategy but wasn't getting anywhere with the real problem at hand, Josh didn't have time to indulge in them.

Which meant that suggestion had been specific, purposeful. He had no idea why, but he also knew Draven was the best at what he did. He hadn't gotten to where he was by ignoring the very people he hired for their knowledge and skills.

He strolled over to the computer and sat with as much aplomb as he could manage. As he'd hoped, apparently the computer game suggestion slowed Brown Shirt down just enough that he didn't react until after Josh had keyed in the reactivation code and the screen had gone live again.

"Get away from there," Brown Shirt snapped.

"Just checking to see if there *are* any games on this thing."

"You think a guy like Redstone plays computer games?" Pinky said with an audible snort.

"Yeah, you're probably right," Josh said, pulling his hand back from the keyboard just as a news ticker he'd never seen before began to scroll along the bottom of the screen. Tagged with the name of a news service he'd never heard of before either, the words marching across the red banner indicated a dangerous summer thunderstorm was headed their way.

"What's that?" Pinky asked, peering at the screen. "Is that for here?"

He sounded a bit nervous, Josh thought. But from what

he'd seen, Pinky always sounded a bit nervous. "Looks that way," he said. "Those can get nasty here. I don't want to be sitting here on this open field in an airplane when that hits. Lightning likes planes."

Even Brown Shirt took notice of that, and leaned in for a closer look.

Then, in the upper right of the screen a window popped open, and Josh found himself staring with some surprise at what appeared to be a business news brief, about a Redstone takeover of a company he'd also never heard of. That was followed by a report he had seen about the quelling of the unrest on Arethusa, a small Caribbean island near the Redstone Bay Resort.

Brown Shirt frowned. "What's all that? Where's it coming from?"

"He has it set up to search for anything Redstone's mentioned in," Tess said from behind him, the first time she'd spoken since they'd been dragged out of the stateroom. "It feeds his ego, I think."

Josh just managed not to let his eyebrows shoot upward; if there was anything more boring to him than reading his own press, he couldn't imagine what it was. He left that to others, trusting them to let him know if there was anything he truly needed to know. And he knew Tess knew that. Tess knew him better than anyone, after all.

Pinky, on the other hand, smirked; Tess had once more fed his perceptions, and thus made whatever was coming through believable to him. And, Josh hoped, to Brown Shirt, as well.

And then a photograph popped up. It was a paparazzi-style shot of a couple, a tall man with a strikingly beautiful, long-legged blonde. It was captioned simply "Billionaire entrepreneur Josh Redstone and date arrive at the Redstone gala on Saturday evening."

Sam, he thought, looked gorgeous in that deep green gown,

even though she'd never shown up at said gala, mainly because it had never happened. Redstone didn't run to that kind of thing.

And the man in the photograph most certainly wasn't him.

Chapter 18

Josh, Tess thought, was not happy.

She thought of the words he'd written atop his list of supposedly necessary repair parts. Ignorance was definitely opportunity in this case, but clearly he didn't like the way Draven had seized that opportunity. Somebody, Ryan Barton she guessed, had been busy with some photo manipulation software.

"Whoa, now that is a seriously hot babe!" Pinky exclaimed.

Tess knew the moment she heard him that Draven had again pulled a rabbit out of the hat; even Brown Shirt was so focused on the sexy blonde he practically looked right past the man in the photo. Samantha Gamble looked incredibly beautiful, as usual. She had, Tess knew, occasionally accompanied Josh to functions when Draven felt the need for some personal security, albeit very low profile; Sam looked exactly like the kind of woman you'd expect a wealthy man to turn up with.

It was the man labeled as Josh who was the surprise. But

the more she thought about it, the more sense it made. She was sure the entire Redstone Security team was here, and if the presence of St. John was any indication, more besides. She wasn't surprised. She wouldn't be surprised if every one of the thousands of people who worked for Redstone around the globe showed up, so strong was their feeling for the man who had built the world they all loved. But of those best suited for this kind of situation, the choices were limited. Rand, if he was even here yet, Tess thought, was clearly out of the question with his very blond, Nordic looks. Just as Tony Alvera was, for the opposite reason.

Even if St. John, who likely knew Josh and his mannerisms better than any man—although if these guys didn't even recognize the man when they had him, they hadn't studied him enough to care about mannerisms—had not already been seen, he, like Draven himself bore a scar that even these two would likely realize Josh Redstone did not. Gabriel Taggert carried himself like exactly what he was—an ex-military man, with his hair still kept nearly that short. And Logan Beck had a similar problem; the ex-cop still had the air. Noah Rider wasn't a trained agent, and also didn't look anything like Josh, and they couldn't assume these two were completely ignorant, just that they were among the many who would never recognize this scruffy-looking man as their billionaire target.

No, Draven had made what was likely the best choice under the circumstances. Not simply because there was more resemblance between Josh and this man than any of the others available; he'd also been dealing with likely one of the very few people he could not say no to. Not one of the triumvirate, as she was, as he himself was, but close enough.

The man who'd named them.

"Leave it to a guy as rich as Redstone to have the good-looking women hanging off him," Pinky said with a sneer that lost some of its impact because of the obvious envy in his voice. But Tess barely noticed that; what was important was that the man had accepted the man in the photo without question.

"Gold digger," Brown Shirt snorted. But he, too, didn't question the image presented.

Josh wasn't frowning, but Tess knew him too well to miss the tightening around his eyes as he studied the picture. She knew it wasn't Samantha who was bothering him; Sam was one of the best security agents Redstone had.

"Is she some movie star or supermodel?" Pinky leaned in for a closer look, focused on the sexily low-cut back of Sam's gown. "She looks it. Man, I'd like a piece of that."

"I'll stick with the hot Latin look, myself," Josh said, startling her. But he wasn't even looking at her, so she didn't have to worry about the color she knew was tingeing her cheeks. She knew he was saying it for effect, but still…

No, what was bothering Josh was the message Draven had sent with that particular photo. The message that they were indeed going to take advantage of the mistake their captors had made.

And they were going to use one of Josh's oldest friends to do it. A man who had once gone through a very vicious kind of hell. A man who apparently now was going to willingly risk ending up a captive again. She knew too well what kind of shape Mac had been in when Draven had pulled him out of that jungle—beaten, burned, weak and sick from weeks of brutalization. He still carried the scars of the torture perpetrated by evil men who knew what the word really meant.

The size of that sacrifice awed but didn't surprise her; no one she'd ever known in her life inspired the kind of loyalty Josh did.

She supposed the fact that Mac had been off the public radar since settling down with his beloved Emma had played into the decision, as well. People's recollection might be fuzzy enough by now to know only that they'd seen him before and connect the memory to Josh, since they'd been photographed together often once the news got out that Mac had been his first—and only—backer. It would be easy for someone who had only noticed such pictures in passing to substitute the one for the other. Besides, Mac had a bit of that same dynamic air. Not to mention he could, when pressed, imitate Josh's easy drawl passably well, although she knew he usually did it to tease his old friend.

And she knew Mac well enough to realize that somewhere in the back of his clever mind was the idea that as a hostage, he was worth as much if not more than Josh; while Josh was known for his planes, his work and the empire he'd built, Harlan McClaren was known mainly for his fabulous wealth. And as a treasure hunter. The somewhat quixotic appellation struck a chord in the human psyche. Especially in those who didn't realize how much risk and planning and plain hard work was involved, those looking ever and always for the easy way, the quick fix.

If Draven's plan doesn't work, he's going to try and trade himself for Josh, she thought with a sudden certainty.

And Josh would never, ever let him do it.

Things were just getting more complicated.

"I wonder," Josh said in the tone of a man doing just that, idly wondering, "if that storm caught Redstone up in the mountains? Maybe that's why he's so late."

Brown Shirt was suddenly paying attention. He shouldered Tess aside. She barely resisted the urge to reach for the weapon, knowing she could take him out right here and now. But they'd agreed to wait, and her move would take Josh by surprise, and surprised victims got hurt. Not to mention, who knew what Pinky would do if shooting started?

The man leaned over to peer at the scroll crawling across the bottom of the screen, which was now reporting some political story Tess would have liked to have thought also untrue but sadly guessed probably was real. It was followed by some sports scores, rolling on until Brown Shirt swore impatiently.

"Come on, come on," he muttered.

Unlike Pinky, the thought of the mentioned storm—which Tess was guessing didn't exist—hadn't bothered him until Josh had mentioned it as possible explanation for their quarry's continued absence.

Finally, the warning scrolled by again, and Brown Shirt's face scrunched up as he read the rather dire-sounding predictions of winds, torrential rain and dangerous lightning strikes. When wording went by accrediting the weather reporting station at the very airfield they were sitting at, she almost smiled at the inventiveness.

"You live around here, right?" Brown Shirt asked the mechanic.

"Some of the time," Josh answered easily.

The man gestured at the screen with a thumb. "Those predictions ever pan out?"

"Sure they do. That's why I only live here some of the time. It gets scary in one of those big storms."

Brown Shirt looked more annoyed than scared, but Tess knew the goal had been to give him one more thing to worry about. The more scattered he was, the better their chances were.

As long as they didn't push him so far that he exploded, she thought. She hoped Draven could read the man well enough from a distance to judge that. But she also knew if anyone could, Draven could.

Brown Shirt's phone pinged again with a new text message. The man scowled.

"You didn't answer the first one yet," Pinky said to his partner.

"Trying to weasel out. I'll answer when I'm good and ready," Brown Shirt muttered, still looking at the computer screen.

Tess's breath caught. She didn't dare look at Josh. Quickly reassured herself that from where Brown Shirt was standing, there was no way Draven and his team could have missed the words. They couldn't be positive the communication had anything to do with what was happening here, but it seemed too likely to assume otherwise. And if he'd meant weasel out in the common sense…

"Get them out of here," Brown Shirt ordered, indicating them with a dismissive gesture.

Pinky smirked at Josh. "Hey, you can pick up where you left off."

Tess couldn't help the vivid image that shot through her mind, even as she told herself that was the last thing she should be thinking about now.

"Come on, get to it." Pinky was leering now. "I'd like to see the show."

"I'll bet you would," Josh said, sounding disgusted enough that Pinky appeared to take offense, which Tess found interesting.

"Just get them in back," Brown Shirt ordered. "And you stay out here, I don't care what they do in there."

Pinky muttered something about taking all the fun out of this, and ushered them back toward the stateroom. She was focused on that last text message, turning the various possibilities around in her head. And was totally unprepared when they reached the stateroom door and Pinky reached out and blatantly put a hand on her right breast and squeezed.

Her instinctive reaction was to take his arm off, quite possibly followed by his head.

She didn't get the chance.

"Remove your hand, or I will."

Josh said it quietly, without any particular inflection, but Tess's breath caught anew. She'd heard that tone from him before. And she knew what it meant.

Josh Redstone was through playing games.

Brown Shirt yelled from the main cabin for him to hurry up. Pinky backed off, with a wary glance at Josh, but with a look at her that chilled her. "I don't mind sloppy seconds. I'll be in later, honey."

In the moments before Pinky closed the door on them, Josh grabbed her.

And kissed her again.

Chapter 19

"I know we need to put on a show," Tess said, Pinky's groping and nastiness all but forgotten, "but do you have to be so convincing?"

Josh stared down at her for a long, silent moment. Was she that utterly convinced this was all a show? Had she felt nothing of the sudden, fierce fire that had so unexpectedly ripped through him when he'd kissed her before? And that had leapt to life instantly when he'd kissed her again? Had it really surprised her that he'd wanted more, that the sight of Pinky's hand on her had infuriated him, and he had seized the chance to wipe the image out of his mind the moment the man had closed the door on them?

On some subconscious level not consumed with figuring just how they were going to get out of this without anyone from Redstone getting hurt, he'd been trying to deal with the shock of this. This was Tess, little Tess, hired when she was little more than a girl simply because she had that magic touch in the air. The girl who had become like a sister to Elizabeth, and thus to him.

But she was also the person he himself relied on. For more things than he could count, probably more things than he even realized. But it had always been a quiet, solid sort of support, never flashy or obvious, simply ever and always there.

You want to risk losing that? Just keep up on this path she obviously doesn't want.

Was even that fierce fire worth losing this precious friendship? Were it not for the pure shock, the answer would be easy. The shock of feeling anything, anything at all, when he'd been so numb for so long.

The only bigger shock was that it was Tess.

She was looking at him so oddly he felt compelled to speak. "I'm sorry. I know that must have felt like kissing your brother."

Her voice sounded strange to him, with a harsh edge he'd not heard before, when she said, "I have a brother. I've kissed my brother. This is *nothing* like it."

"Tess—"

She pulled away from him, retreated a few steps. That alone made his forehead crease; he didn't think he'd ever seen Tess Machado back away from anything.

"You've never been one to start something you didn't mean to finish," she said in that same voice. "Please don't begin the habit now. Not with this."

Josh wondered where all his vaunted cleverness had gone, where his ability to assess, read between the lines and the intent behind words had gone. Because he had no idea how she'd meant that.

…something you don't mean to finish.

Was it just that—a phrase, a cliché, just a way to say stop? He was her boss, technically. At least, as much as anyone could be the boss of her free, independent spirit. But surely they'd known each other too long for that to even be a factor.

He told himself to leave it, if ever there was a time and a place, this wasn't it. And that was a big if; was he truly willing to risk what they had in pursuit of something that might destroy it? Simply because, for the first time since his wife's death he...felt?

It's Tess, he told himself yet again.

That should have answered the ridiculous question right there. The fact that it didn't made him edgier than he already was. He told himself again to drop it. And he hadn't gotten where he was by ignoring his instincts.

Which didn't explain why, instead of turning to what he should be thinking about, he was suddenly asking, "And if I did mean to finish it?"

She stared at him. And for a moment, the briefest flash, something hot and alive flashed in her dark eyes. And although it kicked an answering heat through him, all his fabled instincts couldn't tell him what it was. The possibilities beat at him, anger at the top of the list, anger that he would risk what they had, anger that he would even think about such a thing, anger that he'd forgotten her heart had been buried with Eric as surely as his own had gone with Elizabeth.

That it might be something else, some responding echo of the fire he'd felt himself, was an idea best left unformed. When this was over—and it would be, soon; the moment when Pinky had touched her had snapped the final, thin thread of his patience—when they got back to sanity, perhaps.

Of course, when they got back to sanity, it likely would go away by itself.

That it was the situation hadn't really occurred to him. He'd rarely been in actual danger. In the air, a few times, but at those times his focus was almost clinical as he made the decisions necessary to resolve the emergency. On the ground, only once, and it had been over before he'd completely realized there was a threat.

That once had put Reeve Westin—Reeve Fox then—in the hospital with a bullet meant for him.

And that memory accomplished everything he'd been trying to; put everything except getting out of this with no harm to anyone he cared about out of his mind. That the person he was worried about most was Tess was something he'd just have to deal with.

"Do you think that call was from whoever's behind this?" she asked, moving to the business at hand with almost disconcerting ease; wasn't it supposed to be men who could most easily compartmentalize?

"The weasel-out comment?" he asked, forcing himself to focus.

"Yes."

"Maybe. Kind of hard to call it off once the guns are drawn," Josh said, and unexpectedly Tess smiled.

"It's good to hear that again," she said when he lifted a questioning brow at her. "The drawl."

And that simply she utterly disarmed him.

And made him renew his vow that she, of all of Redstone, would not get hurt.

"I don't like this, Mac."

"I know."

Draven studied the man who was, oddly, pondering what to wear.

All the reasons they'd come up with why the person to pretend he was Josh could or couldn't be this one or that one were valid. That didn't mean he liked this any better.

"We're committed now," Mac reminded him. "Ryan sent the picture."

Draven knew that. He also knew that Mac had a reckless streak, although it had been tempered, as much by his wife, Emma, as by his experience in Nicaragua. It was that experience that nagged at Draven; the circumstances might be very different, but would the memories of the time he'd been held captive and tortured beyond most men's ability to bear make him freeze at some crucial moment?

"Face it, John," Mac said. "The only person you'd be happy with going in there as Josh is you."

He couldn't argue with that; it was nothing less than the truth. He would have been much happier if it had been only him. He'd thought about it—just showing up as the pilot they would be expecting, and taking them both down himself. But them thinking they were about to have their prey in their clutches was better, he had to admit. It would have them focused elsewhere, and maybe give him the edge he needed. Ignorance might present opportunity, but counting on your opponent's stupidity could get you killed.

"Besides, you may be one of the triumvirate, but I'm taller," Mac quipped.

"Fractionally," Draven muttered. He hadn't even met Mac when he'd hung that name on the three of them, but no matter, it had stuck anyway.

"And no one's Josh's six-three," Sam put in, the first time she'd spoken since she'd teased Ryan Barton about his photo work, accusing him of airbrushing her, "so that's a moot point."

"If it turns ugly," Draven began, but Mac lifted a hand.

"Just because I screwed up that once doesn't mean I don't remember how to fight. And nobody brawls better than a port rat, and that's what I was for most of my life."

Mac's life on the sea was legend, and Draven knew what he said was true; he'd learned to survive as a kid on some of the meanest streets around the world.

And in Nicaragua, it had taken four of that brutal warlord's men to take him down.

"Believe me," Mac said, his voice going oddly quiet, "I understand that if one of the Redstone family is in trouble, you're the one they want to see coming. When I was in that hellhole, even though I'd only heard the stories for years, I knew who you were the minute I laid eyes on you. Up until then, I half-thought you were a myth, a story created to protect Redstone."

"Maybe I was avoiding you," Draven said dryly.

"Wouldn't blame you," Mac said with a grin.

Draven studied him for a long moment. Then, very quietly, he said, "I know what you're planning, Mac. Josh will never let it happen."

"No idea what you're talking about," Mac said, suddenly busying himself fiddling with a heavy gold ring with a large, round diamond set off-center in the broad top. Draven knew it wasn't something Josh would wear by any stretch, but they were guessing those two would expect something like it. The ring, in fact, was something Mac had found in one of his treasure hunts. He'd kept it, he'd once said, out of amusement that even in the seventeenth century men had been into flashing their wealth, something he himself avoided as much as Josh. It had been aboard his own plane, along with the somewhat limited wardrobe—he was anything but a clotheshorse—he had with him.

"Besides," Draven said. "I am going in."

Mac blinked. "What?"

"They're going to expect the pilot, aren't they? And they've heard my voice on the phone."

"Mr. Draven?"

Draven turned to look at Barton, still seated before the computer monitor. He'd tried to get the young man to drop the Mister, but so far no luck. The self-described tech-head had the headphones on so he could monitor the situation on board the Hawk V uninterrupted by their planning and preparation.

"He just got a call on that phone," Barton said. "And he looks even less happy than when he got those texts."

"Give us the audio," Draven instructed, and Barton

immediately unplugged the headphones. No audio came through other than background noise, but the video clearly showed the taller man with the cell phone to his ear, listening to something that clearly wasn't pleasing him.

"'Weasel out'?" Reeve quoted, saying aloud what they all remembered hearing a few minutes ago.

"Maybe he didn't mean it that way," Singleton said. "Maybe it's just a word he uses."

"The real point is," St. John observed, "whoever he is, if he truly had control, they wouldn't have dared to not answer when he texted the first time."

No one commented on St. John's full sentence because the truth of what he'd said hung in the room ominously.

"Why did he?" Barton asked. "Text, I mean. Why not just call in the first place?"

"Probably self-protection," Beck answered. "You can always claim it wasn't you who sent a text. Voice contact's a bit harder to deny."

"If he is trying to call it off," Noah Rider said, "do we hold off? Wait, give them a chance to cut their losses?"

Rider didn't sound happy about the idea of further delay, and Draven knew that sentiment was likely in all of them at the moment. They hadn't been trained into a tight, cohesive team to sit around and wait. He'd trained them to do more than just react, and while he'd also trained them to caution, this was beginning to chafe.

"I can wait if I absolutely have to," Tony Alvera put in rather fiercely, "as long as we take them down when Josh and Tess are clear."

For one moment Draven let everything he was feeling into his voice.

"Oh, they're going down, no matter what."

Chapter 20

"Y'know," Josh drawled—for a moment it was a relief not to worry about it—"I've had a bellyful of this."

"I know."

He glanced at Tess, who had been looking out the window on the side of the small, metal building that served as a terminal. He knew her as well as anyone, knew the tough spirit Eric had so admired was alive and well, and many times larger than her petite size.

"You haven't?"

"Oh, I have. But I also know that John Draven has a plan."

"Yes."

"And, I know it's in motion."

That got his attention. And suddenly her position next to the window took on more meaning than simply distraction from what had become an unaccustomed and unwelcome awkwardness between them.

"What did you see?"

"Rand's back. On the roof."

And that, Josh knew, meant only one thing. Rand Singleton had an artistic eye when it came to photography, a passion he'd always had. But that same eye for composition, detail and the scene before him gave him a different skill when necessary; he was the best sniper on the entire Redstone Security team.

The voices from the main cabin filtered through the door again, raised again, as Brown Shirt and Pinky argued. Odd, he thought for an instant, that here, literally inside the scene of the crime as it were, they were the ones out of the loop, while Draven and his crew were hearing every word.

"They're close," Tess said.

He knew she meant to breaking. "Very," he said with a nod.

"If it is being called off..." she began.

"They're in the same boat they'd be in if it wasn't, except without the running money they're counting on."

"We've seen them, would know them instantly," Tess said.

He'd known she would figure that out on her own, that they were a distinct liability on the scale of these two's chances for long-term survival.

"We have to assume," she said, "that when they realize they're trapped they're going to feel cornered."

"Yes."

"They might not actually want to kill us, but they may have no choice."

"And hoping they won't isn't good enough."

"So unless we get a chance earlier, we move when Draven does?"

Josh nodded. Tess nodded in turn, short, sharp, decisive. There was no fear or hesitation in her demeanor, just a trace of relief that they were through with the endless waiting. That was his Tess, all right.

His Tess.

As she stood there looking outside for any further signs that Redstone was on the move, Josh found himself staring at the slender nape of her neck beneath the sleek wedge of thick, dark hair. And wishing he could press his lips to the warm, creamy skin there.

A sudden urge swept him. His entire life had been a matter of imagining and then testing designs, concepts, plans, systems. The testing was as crucial as the imagining, and always had been. Only when the results had been consistent enough for long enough was he certain enough to proceed.

He wanted to test these hot, dangerous waters again.

"Tess," he said, and barely recognized his own voice when he did.

She turned, but for a seemingly endless moment didn't look up at him. It was so unlike her—avoiding his gaze—that he knew what he was feeling was what had changed his voice. No wonder she wouldn't look at him.

And then she gave a small, halfshrug that made every instinct he had take notice. If he was in a boardroom or a tricky negotiation, he would have read it as a sign of surrender, of resignation, and known Redstone was going to get what he wanted.

What he wanted….

The images that went with those words stunned him, and no amount of reminding himself she was the girl he'd practically watched grow up didn't change them. He had the brief, odd thought that he should know her as well as she did him, but somehow he didn't feel right now like he knew her at all.

At last she looked up at him, and what he saw in those familiar, loved, dark eyes startled him. A distinct echo of that unexpected fire glowed there, and he realized that this was why she'd avoided looking at him. She'd known he would see it.

Did it mean she didn't want this, that reluctance to let him see?

"Maybe it was a fluke," he murmured, almost unaware of speaking out loud.

"Circumstances?" she asked, her voice tremulous in a way he'd never heard from her before in all the years he'd known her.

"Only one way to find out," he said, taking another step toward her.

"Testing," she said, as if she'd heard every word of his earlier thoughts. Or, he amended, realizing it was more likely as if she knew him so completely, knew how he thought, how he worked so well that she simply knew exactly what he would be thinking.

Tess always knew.

The old axiom of the third time being the charm ran through his head the moment he pulled her into his arms. And then he had her mouth under his, her body pressed against his, and he knew that *charm* was much too small a word for this.

He heard her make a small sound, a sound that mirrored that gesture of surrender. And then, with the same fierceness with which she flew, she threw herself into this kiss with full, headlong intent. He felt the shift, the change, in the instant before the inferno she kindled engulfed him.

Kissing Tess had been a surprise. Tess kissing him back was a shock beyond his current capacity to measure, and the jolt was no less than if those wires he'd been toying with had been live and he'd been the last link that completed the circuit.

Her mouth was soft, warm and irresistible. Sensations made even more intense by their long absence swamped him, and he tightened his hold on her, unwilling to allow one bit of space between them.

The impossibility of this woman being the one who brought that part of him that had been so numb for so long back to life was only matched by the sudden feeling of inexorability that swept him.

Tess? Insane. She was like a sister.

Tess? Inevitable. Indispensible. Imperative.

Essential.

He felt her tremble and unwillingly broke the kiss.

"Tess," he began, then stopped, not knowing what to say.

"Some test," she said, sounding as shaken as he felt.

"Last chance," he said in turn. Her eyes widened as she read his meaning. He wanted more, he wanted much, much more, but there was no way he was going to get it, not now. He'd had enough, more than enough of this stupid game, and he was ready to put an end to it. Draven would just have to cope.

A movement outside—within view of the stateroom window—made them both glance that way. And what they saw snapped them back full force to the situation at hand with shocking suddenness.

Gabe Taggert stood there again, holding a pair of the signal paddles used to guide airplanes on the ground and looking, for their captors' benefit, like he could work at any airport anywhere. But he was wearing, Josh noted, a yellow vest. He leaned forward to look more closely, as did Tess. For the briefest of moments Gabe looked up, and they made eye contact.

Gabe moved then, dropping smoothly down into an odd sort of sideways crouch, his left leg extended behind him, his right arm sweeping forward to point in the opposite direction. Even if he hadn't recognized the signal, hadn't remembered that Gabe had done a stint on an aircraft carrier, the meaning would have been clear.

He knew by the way Tess's breath caught that she recognized it, as well. It had been a while since she'd done that Redstone-arranged afternoon doing practice landings on a carrier, but she clearly hadn't forgotten the flight-deck signals.

"Launch," she whispered.

"Already have," Josh said grimly. "This ends now."

Chapter 21

"What if they realize Mac isn't Josh?" Grace asked as they were getting ready to make the final move.

"By then it will be too late," Draven answered his wife as he held up what looked like a large, heavy fountain pen. He pressed a button disguised as a gold logo and a thin, deadly, five-inch blade shot out.

"I prefer a switchblade to a stiletto, myself," Mac said mildly as Draven retracted the blade and handed it to him.

"They take too much room to operate. This one is loaded with a special, powerful spring assembly that will let you penetrate from point-blank range." He gestured at the wicked scar on his face. "If I'd had one of these, I wouldn't be carrying this."

"Interesting," Mac said, looking at the pen. "Who came up with that idea?"

Draven flicked a glance over his shoulder at Ian Gamble, who shrugged. "I've taken an interest in useful weaponry of late," the genius inventor said.

Since he'd married Sam, Draven thought. All she had to do was describe a situation and a need to him, and they more often than not had a solution in hand within weeks. And once, apparently, she had described the knife fight that had marked him forever, a story she only knew because he used the details to train his people in hand-to-hand combat. Ian never seemed to run out of ideas, only the time to pursue them all, which was at a premium with little Joshua now on the scene.

He turned back to Mac. "Your sidearm?"

"Ready."

After his near-fatal misadventure in Nicaragua, Mac had come to him and said he'd learned the folly of not knowing how to shoot well enough. Draven put him through a course that would have done the special teams he'd worked with proud. Mac would never be a shooter on Rand's or his own level, but few were. And he was good enough at close range, and that's what they'd be dealing with today.

Draven's cell phone rang. He glanced at the caller ID, ready to ignore it, but when he saw it was Detective Captain Chen, his local connection, he answered.

"Dave?"

"John. Everything under control there?"

"Calm before the storm, which will be short and end sweet."

Chen accepted his assessment. "Good." Then, "Did you say the guy your boss was with earlier was named Odell?"

Draven went still. "Yes."

"I don't know if it's related to your situation, but we found a body in a car, just this side of the county line. ID says it's a Bradley Odell."

Draven was silent for an instant, feeling things shifting rapidly. "Any details you can give me?"

"Not many. Appears it might be suicide. Gunshot to the head. Can't say for sure yet, though."

"Thanks, Dave."

"Anything I need to know?"

"Not that I know of, yet. If I find anything, you'll be the first call I make."

After disconnecting the call, he relayed what the man had told him. Silence descended as they all processed, each one, Draven knew, trying to figure out if this had anything to do with Josh.

"We can't assume it doesn't relate," Sam said.

"It does," St. John said. "Maybe not directly."

Draven didn't doubt the man for a second; one didn't work for Redstone long without learning the man was as close to infallible with information as any human could be.

"Go, Dam."

St. John lifted one shoulder. "General Machine's in trouble. Odell's fault, mostly. Ran it into the ground."

"Didn't they just get bailed out last year?"

St. John nodded.

"But he didn't change the way they did things," Mac said, "which is what put them there in the first place. I knew this was coming from the moment the old man died. He was a tough old bird, and Brad...wasn't. He wanted everybody to like him. So he gave away the store."

St. John snorted, and Draven guessed they all saw the irony in Mac's words. Josh gave nothing anyone didn't earn, in his view, but he treated everyone with respect and a quiet confidence that they could and would give him the best they were capable of. And in return, he had not just liking, but love.

St. John nodded at Mac's assessment. "Vultures are circling, including Carl Carter of Carter Tool, and he's ruthless. And he's got the inside track with the government creditors. Unless Brad comes up with—" he broke off, corrected himself. "—*came* up with another cash infusion, it would have been over. His time was up tomorrow morning."

"You think he asked Josh for money? That that was the purpose behind this whole trip?"

"I heard," St. John said, without elaborating on which of his huge network of sources had provided the information, "he was trying to sell this piece of property they were hiking through."

"To Josh," Draven said, understanding now.

"Who would have said no," Mac said. "He wouldn't put Redstone in that position, not considering who Odell's been dealing with."

"But we still don't know if his death is related to this," Reeve put in.

"Unless he tried to call it off, and when the guy didn't answer him…" Sam said slowly.

"He took the easy way out?" Alvera suggested.

"We can't discount the very real possibility that's what happened," Draven said. "But it doesn't change what we have to do now."

"Then let's roll," Sam said.

They all nodded, and Draven turned back to Mac, who was still fiddling with the heavy ring.

"Emma?" Draven asked.

"I talked to her a few minutes ago. Told her I'd be home for dinner."

"You will," Draven said. He glanced over to where Ian was planting a serious kiss on his wife. He waited until they pulled apart, and Sam ran her fingers through her husband's perpetually floppy hair. Draven was surprised the young inventor's wire-rimmed glasses weren't steamed over.

There had been a time—when his own life had been an empty, cold thing—when he would have had no patience with such things. But Grace had changed that, just as she had changed him, down to his core. They'd shared a kiss of their own a short while ago, and now she simply stood there watching him calmly.

"Be back shortly," he told her.

"I know," she said, nothing short of utter confidence in her voice. "And you will have Josh and Tess with you."

He turned to Mac. "Ready?"

"I am. Enter one arrogant, uncaring and utterly mistaken version of Josh Redstone."

"We need to talk," Josh said, gripping her shoulders and staring down at her. "And when this is over, we will."

Josh Redstone was through playing games.

She knew she'd been right when she'd thought it; she knew him too well to mistake the mood. Josh was through waiting.

It just hadn't occurred to her until this moment that her thought could be applied to more than just those men outside. It was only the situation, she told herself, aware that even in her mind the words sounded desperate.

"I suppose asking you to stay here is pointless?" He was speaking briskly now, like a man with a mission.

"Absolutely," she answered, shoving all the tangled emotions and speculation out of her mind. "Draven would revoke my honorary Redstone Security membership."

For an instant Josh's intense gray eyes narrowed, and she guessed that he was suspecting Draven had trained her in a bit more than the basics. But he didn't argue. Whether that was a tribute to her or to his faith in Draven, she wasn't sure and it didn't matter, not now. All that mattered was getting him out of this safely.

"If it comes to that, I want Pinky," she said, with no more emphasis than if she'd requested a cup of coffee.

An odd gleam came into those familiar gray eyes. "You got him," he drawled, "and I don't envy him one bit."

Movement outside once more attracted her attention. She quickly spotted St. John and Reeve again walking hand in hand, as if still absorbed in each other and oblivious of the jet that sat barely yards away.

Josh walked across the stateroom, looked out the matching window on the other side. She followed, and saw a man in coveralls messing with a cart with several bags. She realized after a moment that the man was Tony Alvera, and the bags were the duffels Redstone Security used, masquerading as ordinary luggage. Noah Rider was back at the fuel truck, which seemed to her closer to the plane this time. A small pickup labeled rather grandly "Airport Operations" was parked next to the fuel truck, and it's driver, Logan Beck, was talking with an air of utter casualness to Noah.

All perfectly normal-looking for an airport. That it was a bit much for this little field would not, hopefully, occur to their uninvited guests until it was too late.

She wondered where Draven was, if he was on board the Hawk III overseeing this operation. Then answered her own question; he would be exactly where he needed to be— with Mac as they started the proposed masquerade. What he wouldn't be doing was worrying about his team doing their jobs. He was as steeped in the Redstone tradition as Josh himself; he let his people do what they'd been so well trained—by him—to do.

She'd asked him once about his philosophy at the end of the exhausting day when he'd at last deemed her worthy of protecting Josh.

"A wise man taught me that whenever one of your team shines, it reflects on you," was all he'd said.

She would shine, she thought. No matter what, Josh would walk out of here alive and unhurt.

Time to stir the pot, Josh thought. Whatever Draven's plan was, it could only be helped by a little internal chaos here. Tess hadn't liked the idea, but had eventually given in.

Pinky, he guessed, was still hovering outside the stateroom

door. So he went into the head, unlocked the opposite door
that led into the main cabin, and stepped quietly through.
Brown Shirt was hovering near the plane's exit door, peering
out the small porthole window, as if looking through the door
instead of the bigger main window would make his quarry
arrive faster.

Josh leaned casually against a bulkhead in a position that
disguised the placement of his right hand within easy reach
of the weapon at his waist, hidden by the jacket he'd never
taken off for just that reason.

"You know, Redstone has never flown in here with guards
before," Josh said casually.

The man whirled. Josh hadn't been able to see if he still
had his weapon in his hand. A shot echoed in the cabin as he
fired wildly, in a near panic. Wood splintered near Josh's head
as a cabinet door took the hit. He felt a sting uncomfortably
close to his eye. Instinctively he reached for the Colt. But then
Pinky yelled. He appeared in the cabin, dragging Tess, his
own weapon jammed against her neck. The sight made Josh
jerk his hand away from the butt of the .45.

Brown Shirt wheeled on his partner, taking aim. Pinky
screeched. He let go of Tess, raised his hands and backed
away. For a moment Josh half expected Brown Shirt to fire.
His gaze flickered to Tess in warning, but she'd already moved
to one side, out of a possible line of fire.

"You're an idiot!" Brown Shirt screamed at the hapless
Pinky. "You let him walk right in here behind me!"

"How', I s'posed to watch both doors at once?" Pinky
whined.

"Just shut the hell up and do your job if you want to get
paid."

Josh didn't miss the contempt in the man's voice. But he
heard an undertone of tension, even fear, as well. The man
was falling apart.

Amateurs.

Josh could almost hear Draven's disgusted voice echoing in his head.

"Well," he said, "I guess we've established you don't work for Redstone. They'd never hire you two."

Brown Shirt spun back around, and for an instant Josh held his gaze, using every instinct he'd ever developed over hundreds of negotiations to try to read the man.

"As if I'd ever work for the all-mighty Redstone," Brown Shirt said, his tone acid, "or any other greedy corporation, sucking the people dry."

"Tell that to the thousands of people who do work for Redstone. So what are you after?"

"Shut up."

"You're waiting for Redstone, you must think you're going to get something out of him."

Brown Shirt's mouth curled. "Oh, I will."

It was pretty obvious now that Brown Shirt didn't care anymore if "Mike" knew he wasn't a Redstone employee. So Josh pushed a little further.

"You know he's got a strict policy, a commandment, in fact. No ransom. Ever."

"We've got that handled." He was so distracted, Josh wondered if he even realized what he was giving away.

"Do you?" Josh said softly, wondering just how they thought they were going to get around that.

Brown Shirt seemed to suddenly realize he'd let too much slip. He swore, sharply, insulting Josh's parentage and species. He gestured sharply, insulting Josh's parentage and species. He gestured sharply at Pinky, with the weapon Josh still wasn't sure he had control of. "Get them back in there. Lock the other bathroom door and don't turn your freakin' back!"

The orders were snapped out in the tone of a man teetering on the edge. Josh knew he'd come within a hairsbreadth of pushing too far.

But he also knew he'd done what he'd wanted to. Brown

Shirt hadn't looked out the window this whole time. And both men were distracted enough, worried enough, that whatever Draven was planning, they likely wouldn't react coolly or calmly.

Every bit of edge you could get counted. If it had only been him, he would have pushed harder. But the sight of Tess with that gun on her wasn't something he'd forget. Ever.

And now it was up to Draven.

He just hoped whatever the man had planned, it went off before Brown Shirt decided to cut his losses. Because if that happened, the next shots he fired wouldn't be wild. And he and Tess could end up dead.

Not Tess, Josh swore to himself. No matter what happened, not Tess. He would not let that happen. No matter what it took.

The group of three people headed toward the Hawk V. Sam looked normal, lithe and leggy and Nordic as usual, although the sight of her hanging—and apparently giggling—on the arm of someone other than Ian was disconcerting.

It was the other two that really threw him. Mac wasn't just walking, he was swaggering. His entire demeanor was one of arrogance. As they walked he was pointing his index finger sharply—what the hell was that gaudy ring he was wearing?—at the man wearing a pilot's jacket and glasses who walked meekly cowed beside him.

And there was the true shocker; if Harlan McClaren as a blustering bully was hard to believe, John Draven as meek was impossible. But he could see the point of Draven looking less dangerous than he was.

"There's our distraction," Tess said from beside him.

"But what are they playing at?" Josh asked, staring.

"They're giving them exactly what they expect," Tess answered. "They expect you—Josh—to be a self-important tyrant. They can't even conceive of a man in your position being who you really are."

He wanted to tell her a little about who he really was—and what he was really feeling—but now wasn't the time. That if things went badly he might never get the chance wasn't something he wanted to think about. Everything else would be handled; if nothing else, Elizabeth's death at far too young an age had taught him that there indeed was no guarantee of tomorrow. So his will, massive though it was with all the divisions, foundations, charities, individuals and other instructions as to his wishes, was up to date. As were his detailed instructions on what was to be done with Redstone itself.

But Tess… No, he thought. He simply wouldn't let it happen. But it could, it might….

This uncertainty was as unlike him as Harlan's swagger. And the unaccustomed feeling tipped him over into stealing five more seconds. He grabbed Tess's shoulders and gently but insistently turned her to face him.

"You know what you mean to me?"

She hesitated, as if trying to read beneath the surface of the words. And to her credit, she didn't deny the possibilities looming ahead. "I… Yes. I think so."

"Double it," he said gruffly. "Quadruple it. We have to talk," he said again, and glanced out at the man who was going to make that talk possible. He'd always had complete faith in John Draven. And he'd never let him down.

Draven concentrated on not stumbling; Ian had loaned him the magnifying glasses explaining that he always carried them because he never knew when he might want to examine something very closely. It fit with the man's genius, so Draven barely blinked.

But he was blinking now. However, having to look over the top of the lenses helped him keep his head suitably bowed as

Mac, pointing in that imperious manner, kept talking. From a distance, Draven was sure it looked as if he were spouting orders instead of recounting his wish to send the two intruders aboard Josh's plane down to Nicaragua for a visit with Omar, the warlord who had tortured him to the point where he would have welcomed the grim reaper, had he come calling.

"And wasn't I thankful it was you instead of the guy with the scythe," Mac was saying, almost cheerfully despite the fierce gesturing.

"Weren't we all." Sam looked up at him adoringly.

"Ah, my beauty, if I didn't belong lock, stock and scuba gear to my darling Emma…"

"But you do."

"I do, indeed. And I don't want Ian to find a use for one of the more exotic weapons he's come up with."

"And indeed he would," Sam said with a smile, and full confidence that her mild-mannered husband would do just that. And Draven had no doubt she was right.

"Josh and Tess?" Mac asked suddenly.

"You're not around as much as we are," Sam said, patting his arm, "or you'd see it as clearly as we do."

"But they don't see it?"

"Forest for the trees," Draven said.

"And a lot of baggage, I imagine." Mac said. "Elizabeth, and Eric."

Sam glanced at both men. "We've all had baggage. Not as heavy, but baggage."

"Time to jettison it," Draven said.

"Then let's get them out of there so they can." Samantha put an end to the discussion as they stepped into the shadow of the Hawk V.

Chapter 22

"Get them out here while I get the door open. He'll be expecting her, and maybe him, too."

They heard Brown Shirt's words from just outside the stateroom door. Pinky answered back. They couldn't hear his words, but the whining, protesting tone was clear; Josh guessed he was tired of being ordered around.

Josh glanced at Tess, who stood at his elbow. They didn't have to speak, they'd worked together for so long they knew each other's cues. He nodded.

Tess reached up and further tousled hair still tangled from his own fingers. Then she quickly unbuttoned the top two buttons on her blouse. Josh fought down the reaction that kicked through him like a mule as she exposed the lovely swell of her breasts above the lacy red—God help him, Redstone red—bra; so much for predicting what this woman would do.

"If he's fool enough," she murmured, and her use of his

own oft-spoken words about an adversary who underestimated him helped him get a grip.

"Any breathing man would be," he said, earning a quick glance that held more promise than anything he'd ever seen in his life. Hope sent fire skipping along his veins.

Pinky's heavy footsteps sounded outside as he came down the corridor, obviously having given in once more. Ironic, Josh thought, that Pinky had it all backward, and was helping a man who treated him like dirt to hold a man who would never treat him as badly as Brown Shirt did.

And then there was no time for thoughts, only for doing.

Pinky paused outside the door. Josh waited a split second longer, picturing the man reaching for the handle. Expecting to find it locked once more.

He yanked open the door.

Pinky, thrown off balance by the sudden unexpected move, staggered into the stateroom. He caught himself. Opened his mouth to yelp. Caught sight of Tess.

A very different expression came across his face as he gaped at smooth, lush curves.

"Well, now," Pinky said. And reached out to touch.

It went against every instinct Josh had not to yank the near-drooling Pinky back and catapult him through the porthole. But he had to trust Tess, had to trust that she could do what needed to be done.

And already she was doing it; he had the briefest moment to see the beginning. Pinky leaning over, intent on what was revealed by the unbuttoned blouse. She took a couple of steps back, as if to get away from Pinky's grasping hands. The man followed, lured by that tempting flesh. Josh was behind him, forgotten. And in a split second Josh had the Colt in his hands.

Simultaneously, Josh heard the sound of the gangway steps being lowered. Brown Shirt, as planned, was focused there, and on the approaching party he was convinced included his prey, at last. In the same instant Tess moved, her knee coming up fast and hard. Josh knew Pinky would be looking at a broken nose or worse. Heard the thud, the crunch.

Josh gave the man just enough time to scream. Doubled over in shock, Pinky was an easy target for the butt of the weapon. He dropped like a stone.

Brown Shirt shouted an inquiry to his partner.

Come on, Josh surged silently as he risked a look into the corridor, *come running.*

Pinky moaned.

Rapid footsteps sounded as Brown Shirt, with an oath audible even back here, started across the main cabin. More footsteps, Josh realized, these from the gangway steps. Even as he heard them so did Brown Shirt; he looked back over his shoulder, torn between his quarry and the captives he already had.

On the floor behind him, Pinky moved. Josh heard a scrabbling sound and a foul, grunting threat. From the corner of his eye he saw the man's arm come up. Had to force himself not to turn his attention away from his own ultimate target.

A single shot echoed in the enclosed space. Followed by a shout of shocked pain and a thud as a heavy body dropped back to the floor. *Chalk one up for Tess* flashed through Josh's mind. He'd been right to think there was no one better to have at your side in a fight.

"What the hell?" Brown Shirt yelled the words furiously. "You idiot—"

It was now or never.

Josh stepped out into the corridor. Directly into Brown Shirt's path. The man's gun hand was waving the Mac 10 wildly as he rushed forward.

"Birds of a feather," Josh said softly, and lifted the Colt.

Brown Shirt's eyes widened at the sight of the weapon. He tried to bring his own to bear. Saw he wasn't going to have time, and pulled the trigger anyway. Several rounds went wild.

Josh's single round did not.

And he savored that stunned look as blood blossomed on the brown shirt.

Bare seconds later, three of the pillars of Redstone were there, taking in the scene with wry acknowledgment. Draven looked from Josh, and the Colt in his hand, to Tess, and the Kahr in hers as she leaned against the bulkhead wall. He gave a short, sharp nod of approval, then knelt beside the collapsed Brown Shirt.

"He'll live, sad to say," Draven said after a moment.

"Well," Sam said with a grin and a glance at Mac, "I don't know about you, but I feel a bit like the cavalry arriving too late."

"But you were the distraction arriving just in time," Josh said.

"I had my Redstone drawl down perfectly, too," Mac said in mock disappointment, but his gaze, as he looked his old friend up and down for reassurance that he was all right, spoke volumes.

"I'm fine." Pinky moaned, stirred. "Or at least I will be, as soon as we get this human debris off my airplane."

"I've got just the guy to handle that," Draven said. He pulled out his Redstone cell phone, keyed the walkie-talkie. "Beck?"

"Sir?"

The voice came not from the speaker, but live and in person from ten feet away as Logan Beck, Reeve Westin and Tony Alvera belted down the corridor. They skidded to a halt next to the collapsed Brown Shirt.

Draven lifted a brow at the rest of the team that had abandoned their positions; he supposed Rand would be here momentarily, probably after forgoing the stairs and leaping to the tarmac from the roof.

"We heard shots," Tony said by way of explanation.

"Don't look at me," Draven said drily. "My barrel's still cool."

The team grinned as one. "You mean, we didn't get to save the day?" Reeve asked, winking broadly at her boss's boss.

"Redstone Security saved the day, all right," Josh said, lifting the Colt. "By all that planning for the worst-case scenario." He glanced at Tess, who looked so relieved it almost seemed like she was swaying under the force of it. Josh focused on Draven then. "And you had your bodyguard all along, obviously."

"I'll refrain from pointing out I was right about you needing one."

"You were," Josh acknowledged. Then, solemnly, he added, "Thank you, John. Again."

Draven shrugged off the praise, as always. Then Josh saw his gaze shift, his expression soften visibly as he focused on someone just behind the Redstone Security forces and nodded. Josh leaned forward to look that way.

St. John.

Everyone fell silent. And the man who had masked his emotions from the world for years, who had hidden more horrible memories than any of them, for one moment let everything he was feeling show as he looked at his oldest friend. Josh smiled at him. St. John sucked in an audible deep breath. Then he nodded, and shifted his gaze to Draven.

"Apparently," Draven said with a glance at Josh, "we're nothing more than the diversion this guy needed to take back his plane."

"We," Josh said, moving over to slip an arm around Tess. "As usual, I couldn't have done it without her."

"If you're smart, and I know you are," Sam said rather archly, "you'll never try."

Draven went back to the order he'd been about to give. "Beck, go talk cop to Deputy Lockner, tell him we have a couple of presents for him. And that we'll have whatever paperwork he needs well before his bosses figure out enough that he's in any trouble."

"Spoken like a man who understands," Logan Beck said with a grin as he turned to go; the ex-cop made it clear every day that he couldn't be happier to be out from under the restrictions of his old job.

Josh realized then that the cabin of the small Hawk V was jammed with people; Noah and Gabe he'd known were here, but he was stunned to see Ian and Ryan, and even Grace all there, anxious expressions changing to relief.

"Tess?"

He said it with puzzlement; even after the worst of crises Tess kept her cool, but Josh belatedly realized something was wrong. She hadn't spoken at all, but that wasn't unexpected under the circumstances. At first Tess had been simply leaning against him. He'd liked the feeling, and now that this was over, he was already planning how things would unfold between them. They'd fly somewhere, maybe Redstone Bay, or the resort in Alaska. And they'd talk, until this…thing between them was resolved, one way or another.

Hopefully, in a way that would let him go on breathing.

And then he realized she wasn't just leaning against him, she was sagging. He looked down at her, tensing slightly to hold her. She smiled at him, so oddly it scared him. And then he felt her tremble, almost violently. And she closed her eyes.

"Tess!"

Her name ripped from him.

Sam leapt across the short distance between them. Josh tightened his hold on Tess Machado's slender, petite body as it went slack in his arms. Sam was there, probing, running her hands over the red shirt, then pulling one away.

Josh stared at that blood-covered hand, unable to breathe as Sam said the unnecessary words.

"She's been hit!"

Chapter 23

"One of the wild shots, it looks like."

Josh didn't react to Draven's comment from the copilot's seat, where he had temporarily taken up residence. He knew his security chief had the most emergency medical experience of them all, having dealt with injuries on the battlefield, so he had entrusted Tess to him and done the only thing he could do. The thing he did best.

He flew.

He was focused utterly and completely on coaxing every last bit of speed out of this plane, praying he hadn't sacrificed too much on the altar of efficiency. This sleek little craft, this child of his mind and heart, was the only hope to save the life of the woman he'd finally realized meant more to him than any design, any plane or all of Redstone itself.

Had he realized it too late?

He couldn't even allow that thought to take root in his mind or he'd be unable to function. And he had to function better than he ever had because, unlike with Elizabeth's ugly, inexorable cancer, he had a chance to fight this. And fight it he would, with every ounce of flying skill he possessed, with every bit of performance he could wring out of his own brainchild, and if the damned thing fell apart from the strain afterward, he didn't care.

"She's hanging on."

Josh hadn't even realized St. John had taken over the seat next to him until he spoke. The man was checking instruments, and looking at his Redstone cell phone screen, apparently at weather maps. He tried to focus only on flying, on milking every last ounce out of the sleek jet. Otherwise, his mind kept leaping into the abyss, pondering the bleakness of a life without Tess's steady support, her wry humor, her blunt honesty. A life without her smile, the sparkle of energy and vivacity in her dark eyes. Without her fierce defense of his time and space, without her skill and finesse with anything airborne to admire, without the constant amazement that he could know anyone as long as he'd known her and still be surprised almost every day by some new, undiscovered facet of her.

"I know, Josh," St. John said softly.

He glanced at the man who had been his good right hand for so long. Saw the knowledge in his eyes, in his expression.

His own joking observation came back to him, that when his mysterious, haunted right-hand man fell in love, he'd know the world was coming to an end.

And now his own world was threatening to do just that— come to an end. Because if Tess died, it might as well.

He was aware that people were clustered in knots in the too-small waiting area. They were all there now; Logan and Rand had caught up, having cleaned up the details back at the small airfield.

"He'd be a good fit," Rand was telling Draven, apparently referring to the deputy they'd dumped the aftermath on.

"And I think he'd be interested," Logan added, "after seeing how we work. Compared to how he has to, I mean."

Josh vaguely registered the conversation, but didn't react. They had to talk about something, or just sit in grim, dark silence. He suspected they were busy trying to carry on normal conversations to subtly—or not so—convey their lack of worry.

Nothing to worry about, Tess would be fine, that was what they'd all said. That was what he told himself. Over and over again. He even tried to believe it. He *had* to believe it because the alternative was unthinkable.

In the end, it was Gabe Taggert who brought it out in the open. Odd that it would be the ramrod straight ex-naval officer, but then again, when he remembered Gabe's own history, perhaps it wasn't so odd after all.

"You're on an…interesting path," Gabe said, sounding tentative, unusual for the decisive captain of the Redstone flagship.

"Until they come out and tell me she's all right, I'm not on any path at all."

"They will," Gabe said, sounding more like his usual confident self. "She's going to make it. She's a fighter, Josh. Nobody with the kind of nerve to fly the way she does is going to give up. Ever. I knew that the first time I met her."

That had been, Josh knew, when Tess had joined in the search for the remains of Gabe's long-missing wife. And it hit him then just how well Gabe did know this path he was on.

"Cara," Josh said, then stopped, not having thought through the tangle of thoughts in his mind.

"Yes," Gabe said, apparently reading him easily; he wondered when he'd become such an open book. Although Gabe was Redstone, and he never tried to hide from family.

"She and your wife," he began, then stopped, still not quite sure where he was headed, usually a good sign to simply shut up.

"She was Hope's best friend," Gabe said. "And now she's the woman I love beyond anything I've ever known." He gave Josh a sideways look. "And I fought it every step of the way."

Josh flicked a glance at the face of this man who had left one loved career behind when he could no longer force himself to ignore the violation of his own basic principles. He saw nothing but concern and a wry self-knowledge.

"It was," Gabe said in a tone that matched his expression, "like falling for Hope's sister. By the time I finished fighting that idea, I was in so deep it was all over."

Every word Gabe said rang true in Josh's mind. How often had he told himself Tess was the sister Elizabeth had chosen to make up for the rather awful one she had by blood? How often did the memory of Elizabeth intrude when he caught himself thinking of Tess a little too much or a little too often?

Gabe shoved a hand through his dark hair, and Josh noted that he automatically started to raise the other hand, as well. Gabe had explained once it was an old, hard-to-break habit, as if he were wearing his officer's combination cap, to be removed before the gesture and resettled after, precisely an inch and a half above his eyebrows, according to navy regs.

Yes, Gabe had walked this path before him. Only to make things more complicated than even Gabe's situation, he hadn't just fallen in love with his late wife's best friend.

He'd fallen in love with one of his own.

In so deep it was all over....

Josh had the gut-level feeling he'd been in that deep or deeper for a very long time. He just hadn't realized it, or allowed himself to acknowledge it for so many complicated reasons. Valid reasons, he thought. Or at least they had been.

Now, with Tess's life in the balance, he couldn't think of a single reason that would stack up against the grim reality that the realization had come too late.

Nobody with the kind of nerve to fly the way she does is going to give up.

He repeated Gabe's words in his head every time he started to wobble. Because he knew it was true, Tess would never give up. And he knew that that kind of unflagging human spirit could work miracles; he'd seen it too many times to deny.

Tess's sister, Francie, would arrive shortly. Mac had gone for her in his own Hawk V, saying it was the least he could do since his copious acting skills hadn't been called for in the end. He'd tried to keep things light, refusing to even acknowledge the possibility that Tess wouldn't be awake and her intense, brilliant self by morning.

Josh sat on the standard-issue, hospital-waiting-room chair, wood arms digging into his elbows. He leaned forward, shifting his elbows to his knees, staring down at the busy maroon-and-blue pattern of the industrial-strength carpeting. He thought that if someone really wanted to make a difference to people in dire straits, they should donate comfortable furniture to all hospital waiting areas. And less dizzying flooring.

As soon as the words formed in his mind he realized how far gone he was, how desperate he was for something, anything else to think about. As if the comfort of the furniture would do anything to ease the agony of people who got the kind of news he'd once gotten, who had had to do what he'd once done, held a person they loved so deeply until the life faded from them.

He consciously tensed every muscle in his body, trying to fend off the shakes he felt hovering. He knew he was tired, the tension of the breakneck flight here had ebbed, and he was feeling the aftereffects. Post-adrenaline crash, or as Draven sometimes called it, an adrenaline hangover.

He waited.

Chapter 24

Earlier, Josh had heard Draven issuing orders to his people, although he hadn't paid any attention, hadn't cared what they were. Logan Beck and Tony Alvera had departed, both St. John—not that he took orders from anyone—and Ryan Barton had set up on laptop computers on a corner table, and Sam and Reeve were on their phones making call after call.

Josh watched all this idly, nothing really able to penetrate the numbness he was feeling. With Elizabeth, he'd known what the ending would be, had known what was inevitable. Now he did not, and oddly, it seemed infinitely worse. There was hope, something he'd finally had to surrender all those years ago, but the not knowing counterbalanced that.

When Draven himself took a phone call and then disappeared, he bestirred himself to look at his watch, something he'd sworn off during the first hour when he'd caught himself looking at it literally every few seconds.

They'd been here nearly four hours. Tess had been in surgery three of those. He knew from Reeve's shooting the damage and dangers involved, and the massive repairs a gun-shot wound usually required.

Draven—from his years in the military—had seen more than his share of such wounds, and had told him this one was in one of the best spots to have one, for survival. Away from anything vital. An observation echoed by the surgeon who had introduced himself and spoken with Josh briefly and briskly before the surgery had begun.

He also knew the operation would take time, that they had to explore thoroughly for any other possible damage that might have been done, and make sure nothing had been damaged by fragments of bullet, or bone if any had been hit; even a nick to the large intestine or an artery made it a whole different ball game.

So many uncertainties, so much unknown. The only thing Josh Redstone was positive of at this moment was that if Tess didn't make it, he might not, either. He'd been through wracking, debilitating grief before, and had no desire to go through it again. Didn't think he could, not with Tess.

And he hadn't told her.

Ironic, he supposed, that even Pinky had noticed before he'd realized it himself. The man's words echoed in his head.

You think I haven't seen the way you two look at each other? Electric, man....

A gentle hand touched his shoulder. He jerked upright, staring into the face of a young woman who looked very much but not enough like her sister. Francine Marqueza O'Brian was six years younger and a couple of inches taller than her big sister, married to a gruff Irishman who would die for her without a second's thought, just as Eric would have for Tess. And had, for all of us, Josh thought.

"Francie," he said, softly, starting to rise.

She stopped him with a gesture and sank down into the chair beside him.

"Josh," she said, one of the few people he'd never had to

ask to abandon the formal "Mr. Redstone;" she'd never used it. She'd heard of him, and vice versa, long before they'd actually met.

"Tess always calls you her Josh because we have a cousin named Josh, so that's how I think of you," she'd explained when they were eventually face-to-face.

Her words had pleased him immensely. As did the idea of Tess calling him "her Josh." And as he recalled the encounter, he wondered if, even then, he'd already been well on the way down the path he'd finally, belatedly—God, please, not too late—realized he was on.

"No word yet?" she asked now.

He shook his head.

"She will be fine," she said firmly, and with utter conviction.

It was the same kind of certainty Mac and the others had displayed. It seemed only he was having doubts. But then, none of them had been down this path before. Even Gabe, although a widower before Cara, hadn't. Not that his situation, with his first wife vanishing and being found dead eight years later had been any easier, just different.

And once again it struck him that the person he knew would understand completely, the one person who could, as always, find the right words to help him through this, was the one under the knife right now.

And she wouldn't be in there now, her life in the balance, if not for him.

He shook his head sharply. It wasn't like him to whine, and he didn't like the sound of even his thoughts. Tess never whined, ever, even in the darkest days after Eric's death. She had wept, wrenchingly, and for a very long time afterward he had seen it engulf her just as it had him, at odd moments.

"The big stuff—birthdays, anniversaries—you know they're coming, you can armor up," she'd said one day when it had caught up with her while they were in his office discussing the scheduling for the test flights of the Hawk IV. "It's the stuff that catches you off guard, the silly stuff, that's the worst."

Josh had nodded, knowing too well exactly what she meant. "I was on an elevator...somewhere, shortly after Elizabeth died. A woman got on. Wearing Elizabeth's perfume."

Tess had instantly understood.

"Oh, God," she'd gulped, fighting her own tears down. "For me it was a stupid football. Some guys playing in the park where Eric played with his friends when he was home. One of them missed a pass, and it bounced right into my windshield. I lost it. Poor guy didn't know what to do with a sobbing woman."

Even then, Josh had guessed what the guy—what any guy—would want to do when faced with a woman like Tess, weeping or not.

With an effort that felt exhausting, he yanked himself out of the past and managed to ask about Francie's now several-months-old son. "The baby?"

"He's fine. Growing like a weed. My mother-in-law, bless her, has him for the moment. And," she added firmly, "his beloved Aunt Tess will be up and around to spoil him soon."

He nodded, not because he felt it, but because it seemed the thing to do.

"Do you know what Tess told me when I asked her how she stood being married to a soldier, and a special-ops soldier at that? How she lived with knowing every time he walked out the door on deployment he might not come back?"

That that was exactly what had happened didn't seem the right thing to bring up just now, so Josh merely shook his head.

"She said 'I try not to waste energy going to meet a plane that hasn't landed.'"

That was so quintessentially Tess that Josh smiled in spite of himself, in spite of the churning inside him.

"My big sister is a very wise woman."

"Yes," Josh whispered. Then, louder, stronger, he repeated it. "Yes, she is."

And for the first time a bit of conviction crept in, a bit of her sister's certainty that he would never have to make the dreaded shift to past tense when speaking of the woman who was more a part of the fabric of his life than almost anyone. That fabric had been torn and mended, was a bit frayed around the edges, but was still strong, and Tess was a big part of the reason.

And for the first time he saw his panic, his anticipation of the worst possible outcome as an insult to her, a denial of her strength and her determination and her courage. And he resolved to fight it as never before.

He didn't know how much time had passed when Draven finally returned. The man hadn't said a word to him about the foolishness of his actions, and Josh knew it wasn't because he was intimidated or afraid to speak sharply to his boss; he'd done it more than once. He wished he'd do it and get it over with.

When his security chief had been given the update on Tess, he came and sat down beside him.

"There's nothing you can say I haven't already told myself," Josh said.

"Oh, I might manage a thing or two you haven't thought of."

"If I'd waited another minute—"

"Who knows what would have happened. You did what you had to do, when you had to do it. You were dealing with amateurs, Josh. By nature unpredictable. And if I hadn't expected you to use them, I never would have had the weapons stashed aboard your plane."

That, even for the new Draven, was practically a speech. And there was that, Josh supposed; why have the weapons aboard and then not use them when you had to?

And then the sense of what else Draven had said registered. He wasn't sure he even cared, not now, not when Tess's fate still hung over them, but he felt he should ask anyway. "Amateurs?"

"Yes."

"So they did this on their own? On impulse?"

"No." Draven's voice was flat, his jaw tight with suppressed anger.

The import of that hit Josh quickly. "Someone hired them?"

Draven nodded. Waited. Josh knew this man, knew what that silence meant; he was waiting for him to reach the inevitable conclusion.

Josh got there quickly for the simple reason that it hadn't been public knowledge where he was going; only St. John and Draven—and Tess—had known.

And the man he'd gone to see.

He'd half suspected it all along; it had been clear to him the man was near desperation. He'd expected Josh to bail him out of the mess of his own making, and when he'd been turned down...

"Brad," Josh said wearily.

"Not exactly."

Uncharacteristically, Draven hesitated. The cryptic response, reminiscent of the old, pre-Grace Draven, also surprised him. But he in turn stayed silent, waiting. And finally Draven, with a wry quirk of his mouth at one corner to acknowledge his own tactic, gave in.

"It was—"

Draven broke off as the outer door swung open to reveal a man in hospital scrubs. A hush fell over the room as everyone turned to look, literally holding their breath. The doctor looked much wearier, Josh saw, than he'd looked when they'd spoken briefly before he went off to begin his delicate work. Josh rose, feeling the stiffness of having sat unmoving for so long.

And for an instant that dread flooded him as the man looked around the room; when he'd gone in, only a few of them had been here; now the room was full, the core of Redstone was here, because the heart of Redstone's life hung in the balance.

"You're all here for Mrs. Machado?" the doctor asked.

"I am her sister," Francie answered, "And this—" she included them all in a wide gesture "—is also her family."

Josh felt a spark of gratitude for the woman who, in her own way, was as cut from the same cloth as her sister. All the while he was still holding his breath. A breath he didn't let out until the man in the surgical scrubs smiled.

Josh barely heard the words, the man's expression said it all.

Tess was going to live. He hadn't lost her.

The tenor of talk in the room changed instantly when the man told them they could see her as soon as she was out of recovery, many of them repeating what they'd said all along— that they'd known she was going to be fine. But Josh simply sat back down, afraid that if he kept standing he was going to start shaking all over again.

She was going to live.

He hadn't lost her.

The world righted itself with an almost palpable snap.

Chapter 25

"Did you tell him about Odell?"

Draven looked at his wife and shook his head.

"Good," she said, surprising him. But then, she did that a lot. Along with many other things that had turned his life from a bleak, barren place to the joy-filled haven it was now. "You know he'll feel responsible. He's not, not in any way, but this is Josh."

"I know. Time enough for him to find out later. He doesn't need to know now."

"Tony was right. He took the easy way out."

"Yes."

Draven stared at the woman who had never taken the easy way, but who had fought back from pain and mutilation to become the vibrant, incredible woman who made his life worth living.

"I love you," he said suddenly. The words, once so difficult, came easily now.

"I know," Grace said with a promising smile.

* * *

Every once in a while Josh would look up at the monitor that hung over the bed, reassuring himself that the numbers were steady, safe, that they said "alive" as clearly as the word itself.

Francie had finally gone to call her family at home to assure them their beloved Tess was going to be fine.

Their Tess.

My Tess, he thought, almost fiercely.

And now he had to figure out how to do this when she woke up. How to tell her, how to say what he had to say, what he couldn't wait any longer to say because he'd almost been too late in realizing. Before, the risk of losing her precious friendship had loomed hugely over the idea of speaking at all.

Now, all that was dwarfed by how close he'd come to losing her completely. Forever.

He glanced around when someone stepped into the ICU room, where he'd been told Tess would be until she was past the chance of infection, always a concern with gunshot wounds. Harlan McClaren looked at the small shape in the bed connected to various machines by leads and tubes. Looked at the numbers on the monitor much as Josh had done, and nodded.

"Tough as nails, our Tess."

My Tess, Josh thought again, but didn't say it.

"The triumvirate is intact," Mac said.

"I've never thought that was exactly right," Josh said. "I've always thought it should be the four cornerstones of Redstone. St. John, Tess, Draven…and you."

For an instant Mac just stared at him. But then he smiled. "Better than the four horsemen," he quipped, but made no effort to hide the pleasure in his voice.

After he'd gone, others came in and out, the whole security team at various times, and the others who made Redstone what it was. All in tribute to this woman who had done so much for so many of them, sometimes to the point of exhaustion, and sometimes even risking her own life to save theirs.

When it was St. John, there were no words spoken, as if the man had reverted to his old, laconic self. The only sign anything was unusual was when the usually undemonstrative St. John put a hand on his shoulder. But when Josh looked up and met his steady gaze, he realized that no words were necessary. Josh knew what this man—who had survived such hell, who had been a kid near suicide on that rainy night on a bridge when Josh had found him—was telling him. The miracle of the change in his own life had St. John believing they were possible for anyone.

Josh nodded; message received. He didn't know yet if he would get the rest of his miracle, he only knew that what he'd gotten so far today would do. Tess was alive, and that was all that mattered.

Only when he saw Draven come in did he recall that they'd never finished that conversation. Who had done this hadn't mattered to him, not until he'd known Tess was going to make it.

If she hadn't, if she had died, he would have hunted who was responsible to the ends of the earth, and they would have paid his own, personal kind of price.

Draven looked at Tess, shaking his head in a kind of awe Josh had rarely seen on the man's face.

"Amazing. So much nerve and smart and giving in such a small package."

"Yes."

"Glad you know it."

"I've always known it." Josh grimaced. "I just took it for granted. I took *her* for granted."

"Some of us need our cage seriously rattled before we realize we're even in one."

And that was about as philosophical as John Draven had ever gotten, Josh thought.

"So what did—"

Josh broke off suddenly; Tess had moved. Only slightly, but he was sure her head had turned a fraction. He glanced at Draven, who nodded; he'd seen it, too.

"Looks like our lady's on her way back to us," he said. Then, with another steady look at Josh, amended his statement. "*Your* lady."

Before Josh could respond—not that he would have known what to say, anyway—Draven quietly left the room.

Josh pulled his chair closer to the bed and sat down. Then he reached out and took Tess's hand, cradling it in his. He studied it, it seemed so small, delicate, the fingers long, slender and graceful, and he shuddered again at the thought of how close he'd come to losing her.

"Josh…."

His head snapped up. And he couldn't stop, nor did he try to, the joy that flooded him at seeing those dark, sparkling eyes open and looking at him once more.

"You shaved," she said as he leaned over the bed.

Instinctively, his hand rose to his now-smooth jaw. "Didn't need the beard anymore."

"I'll never mention it again. It saved you."

"You saved both of us. If you hadn't kept your cool—"

"I should never have let those steps down, opening the Hawk to them. I should have figured out a way to warn you, stopped you from coming on board in the first place."

Josh bent closer. "If you had warned me, if I'd known you were alone with two armed extortionists, there is no way you could have stopped me from boarding."

"But—"

He held up a hand to cut her off, then softened the gesture by reaching out with that hand to gently, tentatively, longingly touch her cheek.

He had thought it would be hard. That he'd stumble, mess up the words. He'd spent a long time sitting by her bed, trying to figure out what to say. And in the end, he'd decided to follow the tenet that ruled most of his life.

Honest and simple, he'd practically chanted every time his mind ran to more complicated, intricate scenarios. And in the end, honest and simple was exactly what it was.

"I love you, Tess Marqueza Machado."

There was a barely perceptible hesitation before she lowered her gaze, answered, as if he'd meant it in the same way he always had. "I love you, too. You know that."

"Tess," he said gently, "look at me."

She raised her eyes to his. And for an instant something flashed in those dark, endless depths, something that spoke to the feelings that had roiled in him in the past—had it really only been a day? But what he saw in that flash of emotion told him what he needed to know.

"I love you," he said again. "You're the one I want by my side, in a fight or every day. The one whose intelligence, spirit and courage I always rely on."

"I'll always be there," Tess whispered.

Josh had built a lot of his empire on his skill at reading people. He'd just never had to very often with Tess, because with him she was so open and forthright. But now she was hesitating, and he thought he knew why.

"I know you loved Eric," he said. "As much and as deeply as I loved Elizabeth." Tess's breath caught audibly, sharply. Josh frowned. "Are you in pain? I should have waited, let you rest—"

"Joshua Michael Redstone, don't you dare stop." He blinked, then smiled. Tess's indomitable spirit had definitely reawakened. "I loved Eric. There is an empty spot in my heart and soul that will always bear his name."

As she so perfectly described his own hollow place, he wondered yet again how he could possibly not have realized how he felt long ago. How he couldn't have realized how endlessly he'd been fascinated by her, knowing her so well and yet continually surprised by some new facet of her he hadn't known.

"But," Tess added, "I didn't bury my heart with him. But I—we all—thought you'd buried yours with Elizabeth."

"For a long time, I thought I had. But it's here, alive and awake again, for the first time in so long…Tess, I love you."

It was the third time he'd said it, but the first time he was certain she understood how he meant it. He saw her eyes widen slightly, saw the faintest tinge of color rise in cheeks that were still too pale for his comfort. And then, slowly, like the sun coming over the horizon on a fresh spring day, she smiled.

"Are you saying you slipped up and drank the Redstone water?"

"I'm saying," he answered, "I've been drinking it all along, but I was too stubborn to acknowledge the effects."

"I prefer the word *determined*," Tess said with a smile. It was one of the small quips she always made that had told Josh from the beginning that she shared his ideas and views, and his drive and ambition.

She wasn't hiding anything now, it was all there in her eyes, in the way her hand tightened around his, those delicate fingers surprisingly strong even now. And in the sudden seriousness of her tone when she spoke again.

"You're sure? It's not just the adrenaline hangover?"

"That's long gone," Josh said. "It vanished about the second hour of your surgery. But…there is one thing I don't get. We've been through so much together, so many times before, we've been in danger before…why now?"

"Your heart wasn't ready until now," Tess said quietly, once more gripping his hand. "I knew that, I've always known it, because I loved her, too, Josh."

That the answer was so simple surprised him, but he

couldn't deny the truth of it. That the answer had come from Tess didn't surprise him at all.

It was only then that he realized that, for all his impassioned declaring, she hadn't said the one thing he needed to hear.

"Tess, do you— You haven't—"

"It is a bit of a cliché, isn't it?" she asked. "You are, after all, my boss."

Josh nearly laughed at that. "No one is your boss, Machado," he said with a crooked smile. "You just allow me to give you planes to fly."

"As long as we have that clear," Tess said. Then she took a deep breath. "But I do need to tell you something."

Josh opened his mouth, then shut it again without saying a word. Whatever she had to say, it would determine the course of the rest of his life, and he resisted the urge to hold his breath.

"If I had died," she began, and he couldn't suppress a shiver at the thought. She shook her head and started again. "If I had died, it would have been with my most secret wish granted."

Josh blinked. "What?"

She tightened her hold on his hand. On his heart. "Your face would have been the last thing I ever saw."

Josh's heart wrenched in his chest, swelled until he ached with the pressure.

Leave it to Tess to not say the words themselves, but say everything they could possibly mean in a way he would never, ever forget.

Chapter 26

"**O**dell is not your fault, Josh. Not in any way, shape or form."

Josh looked at St. John wryly. "Getting downright wordy, aren't you?"

"Liked me better when I never met a full sentence?"

"It had its benefits," Josh said drily.

This was the first time he'd set foot back in his office, and he was only here because Tess had demanded he go; she wanted to whine and cry her way through her first session of physical therapy and rehab in private, she told him.

"It's still not your fault," St. John insisted.

Josh sighed. He'd been wrestling with this ever since Draven had finally, three days after the fact, when Tess had been moved out of ICU and was on the road to recovery, told him about Brad Odell.

"I turned him down, and he killed himself."

"And you did nothing to put him in the position where he felt that was his only way out. He did that all by himself."

Josh studied St. John for a long, quiet moment. "You once thought it was your only way out."

St. John didn't deny it. "Yes. The difference is, I didn't do any of it to myself."

Josh smiled. "I know. Just wanted to be sure you did."

"Then so should you know the difference," St. John pointed out.

"My head does," Josh said. "My gut...not so much."

"You'll get over it. You—"

"Shouldn't feel sorry for him," Draven put in from the doorway. "Except maybe for being married to the most twisted, manipulative woman I've come across in a long time."

Josh drew back slightly as Draven walked into his office. "Diane? Manipulative, yes, and overbearing, self-centered and nasty, yes, but twisted?"

Draven took a seat on the battered leather couch and propped his feet up on the coffee table; Josh didn't stand on ceremony here any more than he did anywhere else.

St. John got there a moment before it occurred to Josh. "She was behind this?"

"But why?" Josh asked. "Money?"

"And anger, is my guess," Draven said. "Apparently, she was furious about what her husband had let happen to her family's company. Ironic, I thought, since she's the one who schmoozed their local politician into granting them special status when it came to getting handouts."

"Which is what landed them in this mess," Josh said.

"Exactly. So she reached out to a disavowed distant cousin who had been ostracized from the family when he got arrested for extortion a few years back."

"Brown Shirt," Josh guessed. Draven nodded. "Extortion? So he had the inclination to begin with."

"And he recruited the hapless Pinky." Draven smiled. "Tess does have a way. Giving your enemies an insulting nickname is a great way to keep them down to size in your head."

Josh didn't even want to think about the little slug; it still infuriated him to think of the way the man had pawed Tess, and the image of his stubby fingers grabbing at her breasts was one he wanted to be soon rid of.

"He's the one," Draven went on, "who was most…helpful. With the right stimulus, of course."

"Which was?"

"Tony Alvera had some time with him before we handed him over to the sheriff."

Josh smiled. That would do it, he thought. The thought of the dangerous-looking Tony Alvera intimidating the little pink man was enough to wipe that other image right out of his mind.

"With what he told us, we went to work on Rich Reid. The cousin," Draven said.

"And how long did that take?" Josh asked wryly.

"Not long," Draven said. "Especially when he realized Diane was going to throw him under the bus, and disavow any knowledge of what was going on."

"What, exactly," Josh said, "was going on?"

"You want just what we can prove, or my suspicions?"

"Your suspicions have a funny way of ending up proven," Josh said wryly. "Go."

"All right. Here's how I think it went down. Diane ordered Brad to approach you. I'm guessing she wanted him to just get you to bail them out. From something Mac said, I think Brad, at least, insisted he had to offer you something of worth."

Josh grimaced. "The irony of that is that had that land not been encumbered by being in the company's name, I might have taken him up on it. It's beautiful, once you get on to the western slopes."

Draven only nodded; Josh knew he understood his affinity to the wilder places, places to retreat to when the business side of Redstone started to drive him crazy. Tess often joked that he'd rather be back in that hangar he'd lived and worked in, with nothing in his mind but the design that would begin it all. And as usual, she was right; he was good at running Redstone, but he did long for the days when the designing—the challenge of it—was the be all and end all.

"I don't think Odell had the guts to say no to her," Draven said.

Josh couldn't picture Brad Odell finding the spine to stand up to his supercilious, manipulative wife, either.

"He sent a text before we headed down the mountain," Josh said, remembering. "A very short text."

"No is only two letters," Draven said drily.

"So…that's when she set her plan in motion?"

Draven shook his head. "They'd already started. She'd had them standing by, although according to Pinky it was a very hastily pulled together operation. But they got tired of waiting out on the tarmac, decided they'd be more comfortable on board. Impatient, it seems."

"Ya think?" Josh drawled.

Draven smiled. "So how tough was it to talk like the rest of us all that time?"

"I have a new appreciation for Australian actors who don't sound it," Josh said drily.

Draven chuckled, then went on. "Anyway, just the day before, she sent this cousin instructions."

"I didn't confirm with Brad until then," Josh said.

Draven nodded. "I figured. She told them the day and place, and e-mailed a photo. The Langston photo."

That stiffest, most formal and most unlike him portrait, Josh thought.

"It's no wonder they didn't recognize you," Draven said, "when you came out of the mountains looking like Sasquatch."

"Did Diane try and call it off?" he asked, suddenly re-membering the later text message and Brown Shirt's reaction to it.

"Not the way you mean. She did try and back out, but she was just furious with them for jumping the gun, not waiting for her go ahead. And for not responding to her communications. A bit of a control freak, our Diane."

"She didn't know Josh has always sworn publicly that no ransom would ever be paid?" St. John asked.

"She's not admitting anything, so this is only speculation, but I'm guessing she assumed we'd override your wishes and pay up. That we wouldn't stand up for the principle, not when your life was at stake."

"Because that's the way it is in her world," Josh said. "Principles are…fluid."

"Yes," Draven agreed. His mouth quirked. "And Reid had very specific preconceptions of a 'corporate big shot' as Pinky put it. How they'd look and act. And you met none of the criteria."

"Story of my life," Josh said, the drawl even more pronounced now.

"Lucky for all of us," Draven said.

"Indeed," St. John said.

Josh looked at the men who were two thirds of the Redstone triumvirate. And finally gave in to the need to get back the other third.

Both of them understood. He'd known they would.

"Are you all right?" Josh asked his copilot.

"If you ask me that one more time, you won't be," Tess answered sweetly.

He grinned. His Tess was definitely back.

"And," she reminded him pointedly, "*I'm* flying home."

"That was the deal," he agreed.

Inwardly he was reveling in the newness of it, and delighted that the change in their status hadn't changed her ability to treat him exactly as she always had; he'd been almost afraid she'd go mushy on him. He should have known better. Tess was who she was, and she wouldn't change. Ever.

Even after this trip.

His fingers tightened around the steering wheel of the Jeep just as they frequently had on the control yoke of the Hawk V on the way here. The plane had been scrubbed and scoured nose to tail, and bore no trace of what had happened. Tess hadn't shown the slightest hesitation about boarding her again, indeed had laughed at the notion.

"You think I'd let those slugs keep me off her? Absolutely no way."

She'd laughed, and he'd reveled in the sound of it.

"It's different," Tess said now, "coming in on the ground."

Josh nodded. He knew the last time she'd been here was to fly in Jessa Hill, when she'd run out of patience waiting for St. John to work through the aftermath of his father's final downfall. It was a good place for that—isolated, peaceful, and beautiful in a misty, cedar-scented way matched in few other places.

In the days of Tess's recuperation, they'd worked through all the baggage, said everything they'd needed to say about where they'd been and where they were going. But it had all been done amid the hovering mass of Redstone, where it seemed everyone on staff anywhere felt the need to show up and say how grateful they were that they were all right. And that they'd finally awakened to what they all, of course, had known all along.

It no longer seemed odd, having such thoughts about Tess. It no longer seemed strange, but inevitable to want her the way he wanted his next breath, a way so elemental, so deep in the core of his being that he wondered if on some level it had always been there. That made him feel vaguely guilty until Tess, as usual, summed it up neatly.

"Guilty is for when you act on a feeling you shouldn't act on. You never did. I never did. Ergo, no guilt."

"I love you, Tess," he said now, rather urgently.

"Back at you, my love," she said, reaching out to lay a hand on his arm as he wrestled the Jeep up the rough, gravel road. She glanced out at the rapidly darkening sky. "Maybe we'll get snowed in."

"Little early in the year."

"Maybe we can pretend we're snowed in."

Josh grinned. "Now that is an idea with potential."

She went quiet for a long moment, an odd expression on her face. He wondered if she were having qualms.

"If you're not ready yet," he began.

"Not ready?" She turned on him almost fiercely. "Not *ready?* I've been waiting so long for this, it's grown so deep into my mind and heart, that I think I will truly die if we don't get there in the next five minutes."

As a declaration of love, it was utterly Tess.

As a declaration of passion, had he been standing it would have put him on his knees.

"How about five seconds," he said, wheeling the Jeep into the last turn on to the track that led to the isolated cabin where he'd sent St. John to dig himself out of the pain his father had left behind. Where he'd often come himself when he needed peace above all.

Where he wanted to be now, with Tess.

Draven took a sip of his plain, black coffee as he sat down across the small table from Captain Dave Chen. He hadn't planned on being back here just yet, but when Chen called, there had been every bit of command in his voice, and Draven knew something was up.

The man, even in civilian clothes, still had the military bearing, his hair was still short, his body still lean and hard.

"I need to know," the man said, not wasting any time in formalities, "what's going on."

Draven had known he'd owe the man a full explanation; he'd given them total cooperation without knowing the details, he deserved them all now. Especially since shots had been fired and people wounded in his jurisdiction. So Draven gave them to him in the best way he could think of to keep the man out of trouble.

"They never asked for a ransom?" Chen asked.

"No. We didn't know exactly what we were dealing with. We still don't," he pointed out.

"You should have called us in."

"You and your hostage negotiators? No, thank you. This was a Redstone matter."

"John—"

"It all took place on Redstone property, technically speaking."

"Redstone property that was parked in my county," Chen countered.

"True enough," Draven allowed. "But in the end, my security team only picked up the pieces. Josh Redstone defended his airplane, himself and his pilot from two armed threats. You going to make a case out of that?"

Chen sighed. "No. But it's gotten more complicated."

Draven frowned. "What do you mean?"

"Odell," he said.

"He needed money," Draven said, and relayed St. John's information and Mac's deductions.

"Thanks," Chen said. "But I'm afraid it's more than that."

Draven set down his coffee mug. Waited, silently.

"Odell didn't commit suicide."

"What?"

"He was murdered."

Chapter 27

Josh's pulse was racing as he grabbed Tess's precious hand, kissed her fingertips.

"I love you."

"And I you," she said.

"Let me get that fire going," he said, turning toward the fireplace. He was stopped by Tess's hand on his arm.

"It's already going," she said softly, and there was no mistaking the intent in her eyes. "It's been going nonstop since we boarded the five."

Heat and need kicked through him. He still wasn't used to the novelty of it. It had been so long since he'd felt anything like it. But he also knew himself well enough to realize if it happened any sooner, he would have felt guilty about it, as if he were being disloyal to the woman he'd thought was the only one he could ever really love.

He'd been wrong.

"You're sure?" he asked.

Tess grimaced. "You're not going to start that 'Are you sure you're all right, we could wait' thing again, are you?"

"We could," he said reasonably. Even as the words came out, his body ratcheted up the heat a notch, and he wished he could take it back. Except that he didn't think he'd have to.

"The doctor says I'm fine. I asked specifically yesterday."

That took him aback. "Specifically?"

"I told him I was going to go away with the man I have waited literally years for, and planned to jump in bed with him as soon as possible. He said have at it. And now you want me to wait longer?"

Her blunt honesty and need nearly took the breath out of him. But he reined it in a moment longer, looking at her quizzically. "Years?"

"Since that day in Iowa, when you slid the Hawk IV off the runway to avoid hitting that dog."

He blinked. "What?"

It wasn't that he didn't remember the day, even if it had been nearly five years ago. He did, vividly; the little border collie whose job it was to keep the rural runway free of the birds that too often got sucked into jet engines—a job the dog did better than any mechanical means man had yet to devise—had gotten hurt and, limping, had been unable to get out of the way when the jet had started down the runway. He'd first merely been puzzled at the slowness of the usually quick animal, but when he realized the black-and-white herder wasn't going to get clear, there hadn't been any decision to make, in his mind.

"I always loved you," she said simply. "But that day, I knew I Loved you. Capital *L*."

"Five years, and you never said?"

"Please. Woman employee in love with the boss? I try to avoid clichés so corny you could pop them in a microwave."

Josh laughed. But then he turned and grasped her shoulders

in his big hands. "You were never, ever, just 'an employee' Tess. You've been like a sister, my closest friend and now…"

He trailed off, unable to find the words at the moment.

"Besides," Tess said, reaching up to cup his face with one of those hands that he so marveled at for their delicacy and strength, "I knew you had to be ready. When Elizabeth died, you threw yourself into Redstone full bore, you built it in to the magnificent, wonderful, incredible place that it is. You had no time for anything else, nor did you want it."

"I want it now," he said, surprised by the fierceness of his own voice, and not talking about time at all.

"So do I," Tess said, her own voice echoing the change in his, and the way she looked at him told him she'd made the switch right along with him. As usual.

She was right, they weren't going to need that fire. One of their own was simmering just beneath the surface, and Josh had the feeling that once it was unleashed, there would be no stopping it.

He was right. And thankful for the thick rug on the floor in front of the still untouched fireplace. He was glad for the battered boots he wore because they were easy to slip off, glad for the way she just as quickly got her own, much nicer-looking boots off.

"Someday," he grated out as they shed their own clothes, "I want to do this slowly. I want to peel back every layer, and take my time about it."

"Someday," she agreed, giving him a look that nearly drove him over the edge right there. "But not today."

She kicked away her slacks and tugged off her lovely, lacy sweater, a gift from the talented Liana Beck, who had also once knitted him a scarf that had amazingly, and only when turned a certain way, shown a perfect image of the shape of the Hawk V.

All thoughts of anything except the woman before him were blasted out of his head when, naked at last, she turned to face him. His own jeans forgotten, he couldn't help himself, he reached for her.

He'd known she was beautiful. He'd caught a glimpse once, accidentally, when they'd been in New York and had been in a suite with a shared bathroom. She'd been like his younger sister for so long it had startled him to realize how beautiful she was, how luscious her petite, curved figure was, rounded and tempting in all the right places, lean and strong in the others.

What he hadn't known was that she would feel like silk and fire at the same time, that the very feel of that impossibly smooth skin would send an echoing fire rocketing through him to pool somewhere low and deep and begin a heavy, pounding pulse demanding more, and still more.

She was strong again now, the scar that marked her abdomen the only sign of what had happened. But it was a reminder, and he touched her with care, lingering on the puckered, still-red mark.

"It's fine," she insisted. "You don't have to be careful."

"I wasn't being careful," he said quietly. "I was…honoring your courage."

"Oh, Josh," she whispered, in a voice he had never heard from her before. It turned to a sharp gasp as he cupped her breasts, savoring their soft fullness even as he realized that some part of him had known, had known they would feel this way, this warm, living weight against his palms. Her nipples were already drawn up tight, and he knew, too, how they would feel. But he waited, waited until she arched toward him needily, before he rubbed them with his thumbs as he continued to gently hold that feminine flesh.

Tess moaned, leaning into him. The silken skin of her belly pressed against him, and suddenly the barrier of his half zipped jeans was far too much. She helped him, in fact, demanded that he discard the rest of his clothes, and they went down to that rug in a semicontrolled rush. He wanted to stroke every lovely inch of her, and then taste every one after that. But her hands were all over him, stroking, touching, and he couldn't think of anything but the stunning trail of fire she was leaving all over his body.

The power of it nearly overwhelmed him. And the sense of inevitability, of rightness was so strong it shattered any flimsy reservations that lingered, leaving him only with a rueful regret that he hadn't realized all this before now, that they'd had to go so long before he'd awakened to the pure treasure that was literally right under his nose.

But now, he simply wanted her under him. Under his hands, his mouth, his body. The feel of her had his heart slamming in his chest, and his newly reawakened body demanding in a way he'd forgotten he was capable of.

There was little of the fumbling he'd been afraid of, it was as if they'd done this before. Yet at the same time it was so shiningly, beautifully new it took his breath away.

"Slow later," Tess said, her voice so low and husky it sent yet another shudder through him; she sounded exactly as he felt.

"Yes," he agreed, then let out a harsh groan as her seeking fingers found him, curled around him.

He'd known it would be good with her, but he wasn't sure he'd ever realized it could be this good, that he'd ever felt a need this driving, this insistent, this hot. Those kisses during their ordeal had been half stolen, half for effect, but now he knew they had only been the slightest hint of what he would and could feel with this woman when it was free and willing and uninterrupted.

And then she was urging him on, guiding him with hot, whispered words of need and urgency that again nearly drove him over the edge. With a tremendous effort, he reined in his body's surging response; they might be in a hurry, but that didn't mean he didn't want this first time to be anything less than his Tess deserved.

His Tess.

He rolled to his back, taking her with him.

"Just to be safe," he said. "For now."

She looked startled for a moment, then hotly intrigued. She lifted herself up, straddling him. She trailed a finger down his chest to his belly, a gesture that would likely have sent a shiver through him if he weren't groaning at the fact that she was straddling him, if he couldn't feel the heat of her, if he weren't imagining what it was going to feel like—

She reached for him then, and with a hungry haste that was delicious she began to lower herself, taking him in slowly, achingly slowly.

"Tess…." It hissed from between clenched teeth as her slickness and heat seared him.

She lifted her head. Looked straight into his eyes. And smiled, a knowing, cheeky smile, as if she'd always known how good they would be together. As perhaps she had.

It was his last coherent thought. Because Tess began to move, and with the same care and finesse with which she flew, she drove him to the brink of insanity. And then, with a moan of his name that nearly made his heart stop, she threw them both over edge. At the first clenching of those deep muscles, he groaned out her name again. And then he was shouting it, not caring, soaring with a wild freedom unlike anything he'd ever felt, and knowing on some level that it would, could only be like this with this woman, who knew what it was to truly fly.

Chapter 28

Josh stared through the two-way mirror at the woman sitting behind the metal table. He'd met Diane Odell two or three times, and he doubted she would ever have pictured herself in this situation. Especially in a decidedly unfashionable orange jumpsuit that didn't go well with the brassier tones in her determinedly blond hair.

He also doubted that she knew Redstone, in particular Ryan Barton, was in large part responsible for her arrest just days ago. Captain Chen's cybercrimes unit consisted of one detective who was computer literate, and what he freely admitted would have taken him weeks took Ryan a matter of hours.

She looked shaken, something Josh guessed was also unusual; the woman wasn't just cool, she was cold, and looking back he saw that she always had been. But now she was staring at potential murder charges if they were able to prove she'd been behind the death of her husband.

Draven stood just inside the door; silently, where he'd been since the once imperious woman who looked anything but at the moment was brought in.

Chen and his homicide detective were with Josh on the other side of the glass, watching carefully. It didn't matter if she guessed that or not, the goal here wasn't necessarily to get a confession, although Josh had told Chen if there was anyone on the planet who could do it, it was Draven, and Chen had seen enough of the man by now not to argue. What they wanted were reactions, reactions the detectives who had been working her might not get. Not to mention that since they were just visitors, and she had consented to see them, she'd not asked for her lawyer to be present.

"I thought when they said Redstone…" she began when she saw Draven, clearly having expected Josh. Draven cut right to the chase.

"Did you have to kill him?"

Her gaze shot upward, but she said nothing. Her muddy brown eyes looked odd to Josh, and it took him a moment to realize she'd had a botched bit of plastic surgery, making them seem to bug out slightly. But it wasn't that he was focused on, it was that in all his years in the business world, in all the hard, driving negotiations he'd been through, he'd never seen a more calculating look. He realized she was trying to figure out how she could manipulate Draven, perhaps into helping her. Under the circumstances, it sent a chill through him.

Draven went on, as planned. "I mean, it relieves my boss's mind to think he didn't kill himself because Josh said no, but killing him was extreme, wasn't it? It's not like he would have had to testify against you, there are protections against that."

"I didn't kill him. I swear, I didn't. I loved Brad."

The amount of distress and grief in her voice was perfect. Too perfect? Josh wondered.

"Uh-huh," Draven said, with a coolness that nearly matched what Josh had seen in the woman's eyes. "You loved the man who destroyed your family's legacy? Who was about to reduce you to, by your standards, poverty?"

"Brad was…"

It had taken him over a year to start to refer to Elizabeth in the past tense, Josh thought. It had apparently taken Diane Odell a few weeks.

"Incompetent?" Draven suggested. "Misguided? A fool?"

"We had the best of intentions," she muttered, as if it were an excuse.

"We?" Draven said. "Misguided it is then. By you."

"My ideas were good, right. He just failed carrying them out."

"Ain't that always the way," Draven drawled, making Josh smile despite everything.

"This isn't my fault."

"It never is," Draven said. "Give it up. They already knew about the throwaway phone you used to call your cousin. Yeah, you paid cash but the clerk identified you."

She'd gone very still, perhaps surprised that this man from Redstone knew what evidence they had, Josh thought. Because she had no idea they'd been given that evidence by Redstone, courtesy of Ryan.

"And they now have all of your e-mails to that cousin you swore you haven't had any contact with in years, and they've been backtracked to a WiFi hotspot near General Machine." She was staring at Draven, clearly stunned. "The proprietor there also identified you. Coordinating those times with the times your assistant reported you—somewhat gleefully, I might add—out of the office was simple."

"I didn't kill him."

Her demeanor had shifted back to shaken, distressed, and her words seemed oddly convincing. And she wasn't denying her part in the ransom scheme any longer.

"You work for Josh Redstone," she said to Draven then.

"You know that."

"If I could just talk to him, make him see, make him understand…."

Josh went still. What could she possibly hope to gain by that?

"And what?" Draven asked the question for him. "You figure because he's such a compassionate man, he'll drop the charges against you?"

Her eyes darted away, and Josh realized that's exactly the card she'd hoped to play.

Draven leaned over and put his hands flat on the table. The move put him face-to-face with her, and Josh knew this was it, that the woman was going to get a glimpse of the man who had gotten confessions out of some of the hardest men Josh had ever seen, just with the look in his eyes.

"Yes, I work for Redstone," Draven said softly. "Do you know what that means?"

Diane was staring at him, pulling back slightly.

"It means I don't have to abide by all the rules cops do. It means I don't have to worry about making a case that stands up in court." She had taken on the look of trapped rat on a sinking ship, watching the water rising. "It means I will do whatever it takes to protect Redstone, and Josh. And to pay back anyone who hurts us, or him."

Captain Chen let out a low whistle; he'd moved slightly and gotten a glimpse of Draven's face. And his eyes. "I do see what you mean," he said to Josh.

"So all this compassion of Josh's," she said, sounding desperate. "It's all phony, like I suspected all along."

"Josh Redstone's compassion is limitless," Draven said, leaning in closer. "For those who deserve it. But you destroyed any chance you had at that."

Draven flicked a glance at the glass, and lifted a brow. Now, Josh thought, was as good a time as any. He glanced at Chen.

"She does have the right to face her accuser, does she not?" the man said blandly.

Josh smiled. Then he left the small observation room and, with a nod at the uniformed deputy outside, opened the door to the interrogation room and stepped inside.

Diane Odell stared at him in utter shock. But she recovered quickly, and gave him a perfectly crafted, tremulous smile.

"Josh! Thank you for coming. I want to explain, I know you'll understand."

He came forward as Draven straightened and backed away a couple of steps.

"It was Brad, I swear, it was. I had no idea what he was going to do."

"I've seen all the evidence."

"But you don't understand. You don't know what a horrible position I was in; I had to do something. You knew my grandfather, you even liked him."

"I did."

"I couldn't let what he built just slip away."

"It didn't slip away. You threw it away," Josh said just as Draven's cell phone rang. He checked the caller ID, then stepped to the back of the room to take the call.

"You made big mistakes, Diane," Josh said. "The second-biggest one was using incompetents to do your dirty work."

"Rich is an idiot!" It was the first time she'd even acknowledged the man existed. Then, as if his words had only now registered, her brow furrowed. "Second biggest?"

Josh let everything he was feeling about this woman show in his face, let every memory of the long hours in the hospital flood him.

"Your first was doing something that got the woman I love nearly killed. For that, I will see you in prison until you're as gray as your morals."

She paled, looking as if she realized just what it meant to have the full power of Redstone aligned against you.

Draven came back. It was a moment before Josh realized he was focused on him, not Diane.

"That was St. John," Draven said, indicating the phone. "He had a name for us."

Josh realized from his expression St. John had pulled something out of the proverbial hat, as usual. And that somehow, it was also connected to Josh.

Draven held his gaze for a moment, and Josh knew him well enough to read the warning there. He braced himself. Draven returned to lean over Diane. Softly, with incredible menace in his voice, he spoke.

"Carl Carter."

Diane Odell gasped, and went stark white. Josh barely managed to keep from looking shocked himself.

"It turns out that Mrs. Odell," Draven said as if Diane wasn't even in the room, "had a meeting with him a couple of months ago. Then another, a couple of weeks ago. Amazing how people like them stand out in places they're usually too good to frequent."

"He himself?"

Draven nodded. "St. John's guess is he wanted you distracted, to be sure you didn't have a chance to help General before he bought Brad out. So he planted this idea in her empty head. She thinks she'll get money out of you, he gets you out of the picture until he can make his move on General Machine."

"He put her up to this?" Josh asked.

"You didn't think she was smart enough on her own, did you? If she was, she'd have picked better people."

The fact that the insults got no rise out of Diane told Josh she was, at last, broken.

"She'll hang for it, though," Draven said. "He's a lot better than she is at covering his tracks. I wonder if Brad suspected, or he simply had him killed to destroy her credibility? Being an extortion suspect is one thing, but murder? Who's going to believe her?"

Diane made a tiny sound. Josh glanced at her. The cornered rat was back, and he guessed it was only a matter of time before Chen and his people had everything they needed.

Draven was surprised to find Grace there when they got back to Redstone Headquarters. And Emma McClaren, Cara Taggert, Sasha Tereschenko, Paige Rider and St. John's Jessa, along with every female who actually worked for Redstone, or so it seemed. All clustered in the courtyard, heads together in that female way that made most men nervous.

He watched warily, until his own Grace burst out laughing, left the group and came over to him.

"What's going on over there? You plotting the overthrow of the government?"

"Might be an improvement," she quipped. "But no. We were just saying that all our practice is about to pay off."

"Practice?"

She nodded. "We have had a lot, after all. Which we'll need to pull off the biggest, most important one of all."

"Biggest, most important what?" he asked patiently, knowing his wife liked to tell things her way, and having learned to like it.

She laughed, and planted a kiss square on her husband's mouth, earning the swift response she always roused in him.

"The biggest, most important Redstone wedding of all, of course!"

Chapter 29

Josh Redstone sat on the battered leather couch that had been with him nearly from the beginning. He'd slept on it countless nights when he'd been barely able to scrape together the rent for the small hangar.

He'd finally managed a place of his own, and by then St. John had taken over the couch. Josh had sensed he felt safer there in the hangar than in a normal residential setting, which back then, before he'd learned the whole story, had been Josh's biggest clue to why the man was the way he was.

And today, better than a couple of decades later, St. John was going to be his best man.

The leather creaked slightly as he leaned back. He was staring at the opposite wall, more specifically at the painting that hung there. The image was both familiar and precious. But the ache he felt looking at it was distant now, far from the wrenching agony he'd felt in the days when he'd first hung it there.

Elizabeth had been a lovely woman, with a good-humored

smile and the sparkle of life in her rich, brown eyes. No painting could have truly captured her essence, not without sound, to render her light, silvery laugh, or smell, to waft that rich gardenia scent.

Tess, on the other hand, had a deep, joyous laugh, and her favored scent was a blend of sweet and spicy that he thought was perfect for her.

"Would you understand?" he softly asked the portrait.

It hit him then, hard. What Elizabeth had said, when she knew her time was nearly gone.

In due time, you'll realize. I trust you both to find your way.

The words she'd said with almost her last breath echoed in his head now, and suddenly took on the potential for an entirely new meaning.

He sat up sharply. Lord, she couldn't have meant... surely not...had she possibly meant this? Had she somehow expected this? Even hoped for it, and in her own way, given her approval?

He couldn't explain the certainty that swept him in that moment. It was as if Elizabeth were there, smiling at him for finally getting it, after all this time.

And as if she were still there, urging him, he rose and walked to the portrait. He reached out, brushed his fingertips over the static, beautiful yet inadequate image. And then he carefully lifted it off the wall. It would go in some other place, honored and never forgotten, but it would no longer be the first and last thing he saw every day. That would now be the woman who, in a few minutes, would become his wife. The woman who had waited for him, who had known him so well she'd known it had to be in his own time; the woman who had reminded him what it was to truly be alive.

Tess Marqueza Machado Redstone. That, he thought with

a suddenly lighthearted grin, was going to be a mouthful. Almost bigger than she was, in size.

But never in spirit.

It was right, Tess thought, that it happen here. And like this. Of all the Redstone weddings—and they were up into double digits just in the past few years—this was the one that would crown them all.

This was a Redstone-only affair, and all the wrangling by others, no matter how important they thought themselves, hadn't succeeded in getting them into this occasion. The guests would be only the people who were most important to them, not the ones who would like to be there for the prestige of it. He might have lost all his blood family, but this, Josh had made clear, was a family wedding. And that family was Redstone. As Sam had once said—more serious than joking— coming to work at Redstone was more like being adopted than getting a job.

Lilith, Josh's oldest friend, had more or less taken charge when Tess had admitted she was at a loss. Her marriage to Eric had been a military affair, dictated by protocol. This was Josh, and she wanted it to be, more than anything, what he would want.

Lilith, thankfully, had understood immediately, and had quickly organized everything except for the venue, which no one could seem to agree on.

It had been, perhaps not surprisingly, St. John who had pointed out the obvious choice.

So now she was here, in the sleek, simple dress she'd insisted on, saying that the mantilla-like veil was enough ornament; it had been worn by every woman in her family for generations, and she needed no other decoration. Here, in the place that was so perfect for this that she wondered why no one else had thought of it.

The courtyard of Redstone Headquarters, with its lush plants and soothing waterfall, was the place they all came to at one time or another, seeking peace, quiet or inspiration. Josh had had the building designed and built around this place, this refuge for his people, and it was the most fitting place for all those who worked for and loved him to gather to celebrate that he'd finally found what so many of them had found.

They'd all been into the office that had been appropriated for the bride, to tell her so, a long string that nearly made her dizzy. Noah and Paige Rider, with Paige's son, Kyle, who treated his stepfather with such respect it warmed Tess's heart, and who talked about his baby twin sisters with a rather bemused smile on his face. Sam and Ian, with bright, grinning, and amazingly well-behaved little Josh in his father's arms. Emma and Harlan McClaren, for whom she had special thanks, knowing what he'd been willing to risk to save Josh. Rand and Kate Singleton, parenthood imminent, laughing with each other in a way that made Tess smile.

Reeve and Zack Westin, who spent their lives ensuring no one suffered the kind of pain and tragedy Zach once had, and who had Tess's utmost admiration. Liana and Logan, who'd had to fight for his honor and their own love. Tony and Lilith, the impossible yet absolutely perfect pairing of streetwise tough guy and elegant society woman, and the newly engaged Ryan Barton and Sasha Tereschenko, sillily happy together. They all came to wish her well. And to thank her for what she'd brought to the man they all loved. Her head was starting to reel; it was, she thought, like becoming queen of Redstone or something.

And when Gabe and Cara Taggert took her aside, and gave her some advice she would treasure on dealing with ghosts and memories, she started to tear up and thought she was going to end up blubbering like a baby at her own wedding.

At last came Draven and his Grace, St. John and his Jessa.

The two women kissed her cheek, hugged her and quietly departed, leaving her with the rest of the triumvirate.

"The best thing I can say about today is that you deserve him, and he deserves you," Draven said quietly.

"Inevitable," the ever-succinct St. John said.

"I love you both," Tess said impulsively.

"And we you," Draven said.

"I will make him happy."

"That," St. John said with a startlingly accurate imitation of Josh's drawl, "you will, m'girl."

With that, St. John retreated to his best-man duties, and Draven offered her his arm. He would walk her, not down the aisle since there wasn't one leading to the small deck that had been built near the waterfall and cantilevered out over the pond, but through the gathering of Redstone, the world the man she loved had built, and the people who were lucky enough to be part of what she saw as no less than a miracle.

A family.

Her family. It always had been, but now more than ever she felt the responsibility of it, and admired her husband-to-be even more not just for what he'd built, but for the people he'd chosen and the spirit and devotion he'd fostered; if anyone gathered here today ever needed help they could provide, they would get it, no questions asked. And they knew it, and loved their boss all the more for it.

The moment she saw him standing there—in the simple but elegantly tailored suit that emphasized his lean height and rangy build—she had to remember how to breathe. But the light in his steady gray eyes steadied her in turn, and she walked onward with so much joy in her heart she thought she barely touched the ground.

The words they'd written for each other were simple and utterly heartfelt, and a reiteration of everything they'd said to each other since that day when time had nearly run out and waiting was no longer an option.

Tess felt as if she'd been enveloped by a lovely haze, and hoped they were recording all this so someday she'd be able to see the perfection of it when she was in a condition to appreciate it.

And later, when it was over and the party—and Redstone knew how to throw a party—began, she looked around at them all, people she knew and loved, shy Cara laughing uproariously with the flashy treasure-hunter Mac, spit and polish Gabe teasing Draven's blossoming stepdaughter, Marly, and most moving of all, Draven's Grace dancing with Ian Gamble, the man whose genius with prosthetics had made her smooth and easy movement possible.

Josh, too, was looking out over the throng, a satisfied expression on his face as he stood on the small deck over the pond, where they'd said the words that linked them forever. The sound of the waterfall was soft and sweet as she made her way to him, through the smiles and grins of what seemed like all of Redstone.

"We have," she said to her husband as he helped her up the last step, "a wonderful family."

"We do," Josh confirmed, looking pleased at the claim of ownership inherent in her words.

"You've built a miracle, my love."

He smiled, a bit awkwardly.

He wasn't quite used to her fervent declarations, but he'd learn, she thought. Just as she had learned to read the same declarations in the way he turned to her for advice, solace or support, and sometimes simply in the way he looked at her.

And, of course, the way he touched her. They'd had a lot of lost time to make up for, and they were gaining ground every day.

"Whatever you just thought," he said, his voice low and rough, "hang on to it."

"Always," she promised.

"Always," he answered.

He kissed her then, deeply, sweetly. She felt the slow build of heat even as she heard the slow build of buzz as the gathered Redstone family began to cheer.

And the mist from the waterfall—that famous Redstone water—fell on them like a gentle promise.

A promise they would keep to each other, and to this family.

Always.

* * * * *

COMING NEXT MONTH

Available August 31, 2010

#1623 CAVANAUGH REUNION
Cavanaugh Justice
Marie Ferrarella

#1624 THE LIBRARIAN'S SECRET SCANDAL
The Coltons of Montana
Jennifer Morey

#1625 PROTECTOR'S TEMPTATION
Marilyn Pappano

#1626 MESMERIZING STRANGER
New Man in Town
Jennifer Greene

ROMANTIC SUSPENSE

SRSCN10810

REQUEST YOUR FREE BOOKS!

2 FREE NOVELS
PLUS
2 FREE GIFTS!

ROMANTIC SUSPENSE

Sparked by Danger, Fueled by Passion.

YES! Please send me 2 FREE Silhouette® Romantic Suspense novels and my 2 FREE gifts (gifts are worth about $10). After receiving them, if I don't wish to receive any more books, I can return the shipping statement marked "cancel." If I don't cancel, I will receive 4 brand-new novels every month and be billed just $4.24 per book in the U.S. or $4.99 per book in Canada. That's a saving of 15% off the cover price! It's quite a bargain! Shipping and handling is just 50¢ per book.* I understand that accepting the 2 free books and gifts places me under no obligation to buy anything. I can always return a shipment and cancel at any time. Even if I never buy another book from Silhouette, the two free books and gifts are mine to keep forever.

240/340 SDN E5Q4

Name	(PLEASE PRINT)	
Address		Apt. #
City	State/Prov.	Zip/Postal Code

Signature (if under 18, a parent or guardian must sign)

Mail to the Silhouette Reader Service:
IN U.S.A.: P.O. Box 1867, Buffalo, NY 14240-1867
IN CANADA: P.O. Box 609, Fort Erie, Ontario L2A 5X3

Not valid for current subscribers to Silhouette Romantic Suspense books.

Want to try two free books from another line?
Call 1-800-873-8635 or visit www.morefreebooks.com.

* Terms and prices subject to change without notice. Prices do not include applicable taxes. N.Y. residents add applicable sales tax. Canadian residents will be charged applicable provincial taxes and GST. Offer not valid in Quebec. This offer is limited to one order per household. All orders subject to approval. Credit or debit balances in a customer's account(s) may be offset by any other outstanding balance owed by or to the customer. Please allow 4 to 6 weeks for delivery. Offer available while quantities last.

Your Privacy: Silhouette is committed to protecting your privacy. Our Privacy Policy is available online at www.eHarlequin.com or upon request from the Reader Service. From time to time we make our lists of customers available to reputable third parties who may have a product or service of interest to you. If you would prefer we not share your name and address, please check here. ☐

Help us get it right—We strive for accurate, respectful and relevant communications. To clarify or modify your communication preferences, visit us at www.ReaderService.com/consumerchoice.

SRS10R

HARLEQUIN®

A Romance

FOR EVERY MOOD™

Spotlight on

Heart & Home

Heartwarming romances
where love can happen
right when you least expect it.

See the next page to enjoy a sneak peek
from Harlequin Superromance®,
a Heart and Home series.

CATHHHSR10

*Enjoy a sneak peek at fan favorite Molly O'Keefe's
Harlequin Superromance miniseries,*
THE NOTORIOUS O'NEILLS, *with*
TYLER O'NEILL'S REDEMPTION,
*available September 2010
only from Harlequin Superromance.*

Police chief Juliette Tremblant recognized the shape of the man strolling down the street—in as calm and leisurely fashion as if it were the middle of the day rather than midnight. She slowed her car, convinced her eyes were playing tricks on her. It had been a long time since Tyler O'Neill had been seen in this town.

As she pulled to a stop at the curb, he turned toward her, and her heart about stopped.

"What the hell are you doing here, Tyler?"

"Well, if it isn't Juliette Tremblant." He made his way over to her, then leaned down so he could look her in the eye. He was close enough to touch.

Juliette was not, repeat, *not* going to touch Tyler O'Neill. Not with her fingers. Not with a ten-foot pole. There would be no touching. Which was too bad, since it was the only way she was ever going to convince herself the man standing in front of her—as rumpled and heart-stoppingly handsome now as he'd been at sixteen—was real.

And not a figment of all her furious revenge dreams.

"What are you doing back in Bonne Terre?" she asked.

"The manor is sitting empty," Tyler said and shrugged, as though his arriving out of the blue after ten years was casual. "Seems like someone should be watching over the family home."

"You?" She laughed at the very notion of him being here for any unselfish reason. "Please."

HSREXP0910

He stared at her for a second, then smiled. Her heart fluttered against her chest—a small mechanical bird powered by that smile.

"You're right." But that cryptic comment was all he offered.

Juliette bit her lip against the other questions.

Why did you go?

Why didn't you write? Call?

What did I do?

But what would be the point? Ten years of silence were all the answer she really needed.

She had sworn off feeling anything for this man long ago. Yet one look at him and all the old hurt and rage resurfaced as though they'd been waiting for the chance. That made her mad.

She put the car in gear, determined not to waste another minute thinking about Tyler O'Neill. "Have a good night, Tyler," she said, liking all the cool "go screw yourself" she managed to fit into those words.

It seems Juliette has an old score to settle with Tyler.
Pick up TYLER O'NEILL'S REDEMPTION
to see how he makes it up to her.
Available September 2010,
only from Harlequin Superromance.

Copyright © 2010 by Molly Fader

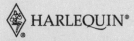

HARLEQUIN®

American ★ Romance®

TANYA MICHAELS
Texas Baby

Babies
&
Bachelors
USA

Instant parenthood is turning Addie Caine's life
upside down. Caring for her young nephew and
infant niece is rewarding—but exhausting! So when
a gorgeous man named Giff Baker starts a short-term
assignment at her office, Addie knows there's no time
for romance. Yet Giff seems to be in hot pursuit....
Is this part of his job, or can he really be falling
for her? And her chaotic, ready-made family!

**Available September 2010
wherever books are sold.**

"LOVE, HOME & HAPPINESS"

www.eHarlequin.com

HAR75325

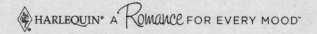

HARLEQUIN® A *Romance* FOR EVERY MOOD™

HARLEQUIN
RECOMMENDED READS
PROGRAM

LOOKING FOR A NEW READ?

**Pick up Michelle Willingham's latest
Harlequin® Historical book**

SURRENDER TO
AN IRISH WARRIOR

Available in September

Here's what readers have to say about this
Harlequin® Historical fan-favorite author

"[T]his book kept me up late into the night…I just had
to find out what happened…I am soooo looking forward
to the next two books Willingham has out."

—eHarlequin Community Member *Tammys*
on *Her Irish Warrior*

"This was a wonderful story with great characters
and constant twists and turns in the plot that
kept me turning the pages."

—eHarlequin Community Member *Sandra Hyatt*
on *The Warrior's Touch*

AVAILABLE WHEREVER BOOKS ARE SOLD

HHRECO0910